PRAISE FOR MARY RANSOME'S
TRUTH: A STORY OF CANREE
NU WEST

"A masterpiece on choices. A gift we are all given. I was captured by the first page to see Annabelle's story unfold. I can't wait for the next book to come out. This is destined to be a bestseller. Book clubs everywhere, here is your next book." Darla Kraft

— DARLA KRAFT

Themes of hope run through every chapter as the author draws the reader into Annabelle's search for more. I was frustrated with Annabelle's stubbornness and related wholeheartedly to the shifting ages of her Caretaker. I felt the joy of Issac and the warmth of the Writer. I understood the fierceness of her Protector and the selfishness of Pedro. I found myself longing to go into the Writer's room, to sit with Him a little longer. And I felt my heart beat faster as the end came into view. Every sentence holds meaning and purpose for a meaning-starved world. Why do we work so hard to avoid surrendering to truth? What might be waiting in our Writer-meeting places that we have longed for our whole lives to enjoy? #give-meallthegrapes #fishbythesea

— CINDY FOOTE

TRUTH

TRUTH

A STORY OF CANREE NU WEST

MARY RANSOME

King Ari Press, LLC; Sacremento, CA 95811

ISBN 978-1-962804-06-6 (Hardcover 2024)

ISBN 978-1-962804-08-0 (E-Pub 2024)

ISBN 978-1-962804-07-3 (Paperback 2025)

❀ Formatted with Vellum

For Danny

CHAPTER 1

*Y*ou don't get to choose the character you'll play in Canree Nu West, and Annabelle hated hers. Like everyone else on her side of the island, Annabelle's Future Book was complete; her story was already written the day she received it. Who was she? She was a Liar and a Thief. She didn't *have* to lie to survive, but she did. Usually, she was pretty good at it. People saw her pretty face and wide-open blue eyes staring into theirs and bought whatever version of the truth she was trying to sell. Eventually, she got comfortable and let her guard down, and every time that happened, someone saw past the lie.

And then she was out on her butt again.

Across the bridge in Canree Nu East, they could choose their path. Their Future Books weren't finished. It didn't matter how their story started; they could still end up as a Protector or even a Caretaker. Annabelle wanted more than anything to be a Caretaker. It was the highest station in the small island nation. As far as Annabelle was concerned, it was the highest honor in the world. Pedro, Annabelle's Companion, was a bondservant. Annabelle was a street urchin.

Annabelle pulled out the cracked and worn leather book that held her future and glared at it. Every page was filled with lies—her lies.

Stories she wove in a futile attempt to make a better life. Every chapter ended the same way; the lies unraveled, destroying the perfect life she worked so hard to create. Her Caretaker told her the truth would make her free, but she didn't believe it. The truth got her kicked out to the street, each time faster and harder than the time before that. *Still*, she mused to herself, *it's partly true. When the lie is broken, I don't have to do the work to keep people playing their role. It's just over, and the work stops for a while. Is that freedom?* She looked over at her blurry reflection in the cracked mirror she kept next to her sleeping bag. *This can't be freedom. It's stealing my beauty.*

These days, she looked a lot like that stupid book—cracked, worn, frayed around the edges. It had been a lot easier to pull people into her story when she was a teenager, when her pale skin looked like fine china, and her bright blue eyes stood out in perfect contrast to her perfect dark hair. Back then, it fluttered and flowed instead of crackling from too many times of being dyed. Checking out her hair in the mirror, she realized it was time to dye it again. She enjoyed the golden color of this last con, but a new chapter called for a new hair color—maybe a red this time.

She remembered the day they handed her the brand-new Future Book. Its leather was soft, and the pages crackled as she spread it open. It held such promise back then. The elegant script fascinated her. She had been too young to read it, but late at night, as she curled up in her box and looked out the slit into the night sky, she imagined herself gliding through the chapters of her life like the dark slanted letters slid effortlessly across the page. Her life would be magical and perfect. Her Companion would be tall and handsome, with deep brown eyes, dark hair, and skin that shimmered a deep brown. One day, she and her Companion would sail away from this place. She imagined the markings moving like the waves on the ocean that surrounded them. The markings seemed graceful and happy once upon a time, but looking at them now, she thought they looked like snakes. They weren't waving across the page anymore; they slithered. She hated them like she hated herself. Like she hated everyone.

Annabelle thought back to the first time she tried to change her story. It wasn't long after she learned to read the strange lettering. She devoured her story as quickly as she could, scanning page after page, looking for something, anything to give her hope. But she didn't know what she was looking for, and ultimately, she didn't find it. She saw that her life would not get better, and there was no ship to take her away from her fate. Her Companion *would* be tall and handsome, and for a moment, she was satisfied. As she continued to read, however, she saw that his looks covered a dark heart. When she reached the end of her book, Annabelle sobbed and screamed. She ran then to the Keeper's court, where the giant, stone-faced being monitored and directed the course of human lives. As far as Annabelle knew, the being had never moved once, choosing instead to send his Messenger out to do the work. And for some reason, he let the Writer be the creator of the books. The Keeper just somehow kept things moving in the direction he had chosen before the island even existed.

In her rush, Annabelle plowed directly into the Messenger in the outer courtyard. The Messenger was a small feminine being that seemed to float rather than walk or run. Even though Annabelle slammed into her at a full run, the Messenger's touch felt like a gentle nudge. Annabelle seized her chance and asked, "Can you take a message to the Keeper?" In response, the Messenger handed her an envelope. The card inside simply said, "Truth."Annabelle shoved it hastily into her pocket and repeated, "About that message?" The Messenger shook her head and pointed to the pocketed card. "Truth," she said in a calm and quiet voice. Annabelle's voice was harsh and abrasive as she cried out, "Can you or can you not get a message to the Keeper for me!?"

"The only message the Keeper has for you, I have already given." Annabelle watched her lips form the word "truth" once again but couldn't hear the sound. Impatient with the delay, she pushed past the Messenger and into the Keeper's court.

Annabelle remembered the Keeper's inner space felt cool compared to the heat of the day. It was darker than the outer court, and it took a moment for her eyes to adjust. When they did, she realized she was looking directly at the Keeper, but even though she was gazing high above her, what she saw was the rich textures of his multi-colored coat. Looking up at an even sharper angle, she saw his icy gaze, always facing one direction. Never moving. If Annabelle hadn't seen the subtle motion of his shoulders as he breathed, she would have assumed it was simply a statue like the copper one in the center square. Looking around, Annabelle realized that the center square was a copy of the space she saw here. Wide open with fire and fountains and carefully chosen flowers surrounding the Keeper, who sat on what could only be described as a throne. Behind the Keeper and to the left, there was a desk. It was imposing enough, but the Keeper dwarfed the desk and the Writer who sat there.

Remembering why she was there—the horror of the story written for her—Annabelle spoke in a loud, clear voice that shattered the solemnity of the inner space. "This can't be my story. This can't be how it ends! I need you to change it."

She got no response from the stony, cold face. She looked to the Writer with his head bowed low over a page. He was hidden in the Keeper's shadow as he wrote another Future Book. She wondered for a moment if he could change hers, but he was thoroughly absorbed in his work and didn't look up. As she watched, a drop of dark sweat fell from the Writer's head to the page he was working on. It must've been someone's last page because he wiped his forehead and closed the book, handing it to the Messenger.

As Annabelle thought back to that day, she remembered the cavernous feeling of the room and how it mirrored the feeling inside of her. She didn't know what to do. The quiet hum of the room had resumed without anyone glancing in her direction. She was invisible in this place of greatness, a worthless street urchin with no say in the course of her life. The helplessness of the life laid out for her in the small leather-bound book sparked a dark rage deep inside her. It blurred her vision until the colors of the Keeper's coat mixed with the flowers and the flames. She could not; she *would not* accept this story she never asked for. Her eyes slowly focused on her Future Book, clasped in her hand. The book was the problem. The fire on her left caught her eye. Annabelle remembered Caretaker telling her about a time she witnessed two people walk through the fire at the bidding of the Three. The first person made it through the fire with his clothes not only intact but also made white. The second made it through, but her clothes were blackened and smoking. Caretaker cried when she told Annabelle. Caretaker didn't cry, ever, so the story stuck with Annabelle. *Maybe the fire would change the Future Book too.*

Annabelle recklessly flung her Future Book into the fire. The low murmur of the thoughts between the Keeper, Writer, and Messenger suddenly stopped, and the silence screamed louder than Annabelle had moments before. All motion in the room was stilled as sparks flew out from the center of the fire. Annabelle felt rather than saw the Messenger move toward it. She reached in, peace written across her face, and retrieved the book from the flames. She handed the smoking book back to Annabelle with one more murmured reminder to read her message and returned to stand ready near the Writer. Annabelle flipped the book open, frantically searching the pages for any sign of a change, but the only thing was the book now reeked of smoke. *Great.*

She turned her attention to the center fountain. A single shoot of water, straight up in the air and returning again upon itself to a pool of cloudy water. Annabelle had heard stories of the pool as well—how weak people would walk under the spray and find strength. Dirty ones would be washed clean. And the sick would find the sickness gone when they passed through to the other side. Annabelle was pretty sure most of it was just fabricated from the imaginations of people too desperate to see that it was just water. But just in case she was wrong, she threw the Book into the water. Again, she felt the prickly and shocked silence of the inner space. The Messenger looked to the Writer, who looked to the Keeper. The Writer must've seen something that Annabelle missed; all she saw was the same stony face she had seen when she walked in, but the Writer nodded and stood. He walked through the fountain and handed her the book. The Future Book was soaked all the way through, but it remained unchanged. Annabelle cried out from the depths of rage inside her, screaming in helpless despair.

Then she opened the book and ripped out a page.

The Keeper turned one eye toward her, filling her with terror. The page she pulled from the Book burst into flame in her hand, burning her palm and leaving behind a white marking. Unsure how she knew, Annabelle immediately felt that the marking meant something; she just didn't know what. Since then, she had seen it twice on other people's hands. One was an older man with jet-black hair and soft brown eyes. Sad eyes. She met him in the market when she had just been kicked out of another home. She was working on building her next story when she got hungry and headed to the market to steal some food. She was distracted and angry, and she got sloppy. He caught her as she yanked a bunch of grapes off his booth, but when he saw her marked hand, he let her go and dismissed her with a curt nod. She stared at him just long enough to see a tear fall down his cheek as he opened his own marked palm to her. Then she took off running. His face still haunted her dreams. She threw the grapes away.

The other person with the mark was her Caretaker. But Caretaker didn't have just the one white mark in the middle of her palm. She had many marks all over her body in all different colors. It seemed every part of her had another mysterious letter burned into her. Annabelle asked her about the marks, but the Caretaker never answered her questions with anything more than a "You'll see someday. And when you do, remember what I told you." Annabelle hated the Caretaker. And the Keeper. And the stupid Future Book. She hadn't looked inside the book since the moment she tore out the page. She just ran out of the inner space, through the outer court, and into the city beyond. She kept running until she found her box and her sleeping bag. Throwing herself into it, she wept.

Annabelle's thoughts came back to the present as she shook herself free of the memory. She was back on that same old sleeping bag in the same old box. Both showed the years of wear that were evident on her face. She looked away from the broken mirror to the cracked book. She carried the book with her everywhere she went but never opened it. She never even pulled it out except on days like today— milestone days. The days that said time were still marching on, and she hadn't found a way to rewrite her story yet. Every word written in the book had burned itself inside of her brain. She saw the ending every time she closed her eyes. It was why she couldn't sleep. And since she had to sleep but couldn't, it was also why she drank. Dropping the cracked, smoke-drenched book back into her bag, she fumbled around until she found the flask she was looking for. Not much left, but it was better than nothing.

Whenever she was rejected again, she found her way back to her first box. It was crumbling, but her box still stood where it always had, in the alley behind a row of attached shops. Hers wasn't the only box there, but she had a prime spot in between two of the shops' back doors. And since the shops had been abandoned long ago, there was no one to use the doors.

Pedro didn't understand why she kept going back to her box. But it felt more like home than anywhere else she had ever lived. The print on the outside of the box had long since faded. The sides and top gave her a confined, secure feeling whenever the world got too big and out of control. Early on in her time there, she had cut a slit into the top. Not large, just enough to see the sky. She would lay back on her musty sleeping bag and stare through the slit, hoping to see a shooting star so she could make a wish.

This box was her home until she was six years old and given to Caretaker and Protector. Annabelle's Caretaker was either very young or very old; Annabelle couldn't tell. Her Caretaker was like one of those pictures that changed depending on the angle from which you saw it. Annabelle asked her once how old she was, but the Caretaker's response just made her more confused. She said, "I'm almost as old as I need to be but always as young as I can be." Caretaker was always saying strange things. However old she got, Caretaker did have one thing that always made her shift back to the younger version. She sometimes went away by herself with her Future Book and another very old book. Annabelle never knew where she went, but when she came back, the light was back in her eyes, and she appeared years younger.

Annabelle's Protector, unlike her Caretaker, was always direct. She didn't see her Protector often—he was always out doing Protector things—but when he did show up, it was like he could see right through her. She tried to lie to him, but it never worked. She could get things past the Caretaker. It was almost too easy. But never the Protector. Everyone always looked at Annabelle's Protector with awe. He was large. Very large. Annabelle knew he wasn't as big as he looked, but she could never explain that to the people who saw him. Even Pedro was afraid of him. Protector's eyes were wise but sad and a clear, piercing blue. Sometimes, people would compare Annabelle's eyes to his. Well, they used to anyway. The gray at his temples looked so much a part of him as if it had always been there. Maybe it had. Her Protector was the highest-ranked Protector on the island. Annabelle didn't really understand—with a story like hers, why would it matter who protected her?

The story written in Annabelle's Future Book began the day she was given to Caretaker and Protector. It was separated into Chapters and Days. Each new con began a new chapter, and each chapter ended the same. She got caught. She got rejected. She got tossed out with the other trash. And the cycle started again. Chapter one began the day she moved in. It was really a practice run where she worked out the bugs for the future. She pretended to be doing everything Caretaker and Protector told her to, but in reality, she was doing the opposite. Every time. *That was not my best work. Still, it was a start.* Protector always found the things she tried to hide. Sometimes, she could prevail upon Caretaker to be on her side by twisting and contorting the lies until it looked like she was right and Protector was wrong. It worked really well on the days that Caretaker looked old. And whenever it did work, Caretaker got older.

Eventually, she left the Caretaker and Protector. It wasn't that she really wanted to… but it was written at the end of Chapter One. Day 4,382. She walked out and never looked back. That's what her Future Book said she would do, so she did.

There weren't a lot of chapters in her book. There was the one where she actually got hired on to look after some of the young orphans for the Keeper. Not as a Caretaker, but it was a first step toward what she wanted. She had watched her Caretaker carefully—

obsessively. And she knew if she could choose her own story, that would be the path she would take. She knew she could never get there with the truth of who she was. She wasn't exactly running a con on the Keeper since no one ever could. But she ran it on all the suckers who followed him. She dressed in the same uniform and pasted a smile on her face. Pedro ruined that con for her the day he visited her at the children's home. He wouldn't wait for her to get off work and get to the rendezvous point where they could take their time. He took her inside a cleaning closet where the janitor walked in. It wouldn't be so bad, but the janitor had been paying attention and could tell Annabelle wasn't what she said. He took them directly to the head of the district and exposed them. She was thrown out. Chapter Two, Day 476. The cons weren't the same length, so the chapters weren't either. Chapter Two was one of the longer ones. Her cons were always well-planned and almost flawlessly executed. Almost.

Every moment of every day felt like deja vu for Annabelle. When she read her Future Book at twelve years old, the words became a part of her. Even when she screwed up at the end of *every con* and got caught—she knew what the screwup would be. She saw it coming, but she couldn't do a thing about it. She almost believed at that moment that she could pull it off after all. That the book didn't really determine her future and she could make the choice. She was always wrong.

She met Pedro in Chapter One. Day 2,879. She knew he would be "trouble" until her final day, but she couldn't walk away from him. She didn't want to. He was everything she ever wanted. And he wanted her, too, at least in the beginning. It didn't take too many cons for him to figure out he was being conned, too… but he was as stuck as she and couldn't walk away from her either. Their Future Books kept them side by side until the last page of her last chapter. She shuddered, thinking about the final words. They slithered across her vision like living things, taunting her with their inevitability, their finality.

Chapter 6 —Day 12.

9

You drop your bloodied knife moments before you black out and land on it. You will not wake up the next day.

Her current chapter was disrupted earlier that day when she was kicked out of the Governor's house. They caught her in the act of stealing one of the larger paintings. She knew better. She knew the Governor's youngest son would be sick that day, causing his Nanny to be walking down that particular corridor at just the right time to find her instead of out at the park as scheduled. She knew but she was stuck in this narrative she didn't choose. She cursed the Keeper in her mind for dooming her to a life of failure and, ultimately, death. Her final moments hung heavily over her tonight. Suddenly, the few drops of whiskey she had left weren't enough. She knew if she headed out now, she could find an open bar. She had to have another drink. Anyway, there was no point in fighting the urge now; that's how it was written in the book.

CHAPTER 2

Chapter 6—Day 1
You don't remember falling asleep, but when the sun hits your eyes, you know you must have.

Annabelle opened one eye slowly and saw the sun gleaming through the slit on the top of the box. UGH. She saw the page in her mind. Today, she will steal pineapple on her way through the market. She didn't want to work. If the book was right, she would never want to work again. And the book was always right, so she wouldn't be working. That left sitting by the river and prepping the next con. *But why? When I know I won't even make it to the beginning?* But as she shoved her sleeping bag back into a heap in the corner, she knew she couldn't do anything that wasn't in the book. And she HAD to do what was there.

You kick the sleeping bag back into its corner, and a wave of despair washes over you.

Keeper, I'm so freaking predictable. She screamed as she kicked it. With only eleven days left, she wasn't any closer to changing her fate than she had been the day she tore out the page. The story stayed the same. She knew the future as well as she knew her memories. She knew what the next eleven days held as if she had already lived them. And she knew how it would end.

You climb out of your box and stretch. Despite your foul mood, you breathe in deeply. The salty sea air refreshes you. The breeze softens the warmth of the sun. You're tempted to see the good in the day but your doom hangs over you and won't allow peace to reside for long. You impatiently brush aside any feelings of peace as you decide that if you're going to die, you might as well get yourself one hell of a breakfast. You might even pay for it today. You glance at your jar of coins and bills. There's no way you'll ever get off this island now. You're still thousands shy of the cost of passage to the mainland. You might as well give up. Shrugging, you decide to head toward the docks and see if you can swipe some fresh pineapple. The little stands nearest the boardwalk hold the freshest and nicest fruits.

As Annabelle headed toward the docks, she contemplated the trip to the mainland she always wanted to take. She didn't know what was over there, but the tourists who came by the shipload always looked so happy and relaxed. She dreamed of being clothed like they were and covered in jewels. She was still thousands shy of her goal. Stealing her food every day cut down on costs but it seemed every con took more initial investment and Pedro kept demanding more and more of the take.

She reached the docks and saw a stand with fresh mangoes nearby. The owner was distracted, fawning over a wealthy customer, helping them choose the very best produce. It would be so easy to take a mango or two. Annabelle stretched out her arm to grab one, then remembered that it was written that she would take pineapple. She looked longingly at the mango and walked on by. She saw another stand and angled herself toward it. The owner was older and losing his sight. She made short work of distracting him and swiping the strips of pineapple, then moved toward the river and her bridge.

The space under the bridge is your safe place. You head there with your pineapple and find your folding beach chair tucked away in a crevice. You drop your Future Book, pull out the chair and flop unceremoniously into it, thinking about how proper you had to be at the governor's house and how perhaps you'll try something simpler for your next con. You contemplate your next choice as you stare at the river. The river feels a lot like your life—dull and motionless. But looking at the other side of the river gives you an idea...

Annabelle dropped her Future Book on the ground and flopped into her chair exactly how the book said she would—thinking about how nice it was to simply be herself and not worry about doing something inappropriate for the stiff and fancy governor's mansion. Ugh, how she hated that place and all the people in it. They were so easy to manipulate with a detached air and lifted nose. If only she had been able to make that last big score, she'd be much happier sitting in her crappy chair by the muddy water. The water felt so lifeless and stale today. It was getting places about as quickly as she was. She stuck out her tongue at the thought. Life on this side of the island wasn't worth the space it took up. She melted down in her chair and looked back at the drab, low-profile buildings that made up most of the city. Of course, down by the docks, there were flamboyant colors and artificial culture designed to delight and impress the cruise passengers. But over here, on the other side of the brightly painted walls, nothing looked like that. It was all business as usual and pretty hopeless business at that. She turned back, munching on another slice of pineapple but still feeling rather salty over the fact that she was eating pineapple instead of the luscious mango she had seen at the first booth. The book left her no joy in life. Every step is planned ahead. Every thought and action is chosen for her, and no way to alter the narrative! She threw the remaining pineapple passionately into the river and watched it hit the water with a very unsatisfying plop.

In the water, she caught the murky reflection of the buildings across the way and looked up at them. Unlike the west side of Canree Nu, the east side seemed to be prospering. Tall, beautiful buildings with wide windows displaying the potted greenery inside plush offices. *Plants. Inside buildings. Not even the governor's house could afford that kind of luxury over here.* Down where the river curved, a Caretaker had three small children on a picnic blanket. The laughing, perfect children brought the Caretaker tiny flowers they found growing near the bank.

They get to write their own story.

The thought came with a shiver as a cloud passed over where she sat. For a second, she felt a shudder of fear wash through her body, but then the cloud moved on, and the moment passed. Looking down, she realized there was an envelope in her hand. *I wonder where this came from.* Shrugging, she opened it, hoping it said something more interesting than "Truth," like the last message.

You deserve a different ending.

She *did* deserve a different ending than the one that haunted her continually. Nobody deserved an ending that bad! She pulled out the other message, the one that just said "Truth." She looked at both cards, feeling like there was something different about this second one. It took a minute, but she realized that the ink on the new card was shimmering. *Maybe the old one had a shimmer, but it got rubbed off.* She pushed away the uneasy feeling that something was off with the new card. It looked like something the Writer would say, and it came on the same kind of card. It must be from him. Anyway, she liked this message a LOT more than the first one. *What the hell is Truth anyway? Truth is what you make it.*

She tucked both cards into her pocket and looked at the happy little kids across the water again. If only she had been born over there. They had everything they could ever want, and even the pathetic little wildflowers made them dance and giggle. She deserved the same life they get to have. Indignation rose inside of her, and with it, the form of a plan began to emerge.

You decide that the only way to create your own ending is to get to the East side of Canre Nu. Sneering at the leather book, you contemplate throwing it into the muddy water along with your uneaten pineapple, but you really don't want another visit from the Messenger. Or, Keeper forbid, the Writer! What had he ever done for you anyway? Why should you finish out the horrible play he wrote for you? No! It's time to find your own way now. Today. Just as you're about to stand up and swim across the giant muddy river, a rock skips down the slope and taps your foot. Only one other person comes this way: Pedro.

Pedro towered over Annabelle's tall, slender frame. He had intense brown eyes and dark, wavy hair. He was just the kind of guy

Annabelle had always dreamed of having for her Companion. For half a second, Annabelle was drawn back to the very first time they met, when Pedro walked into a party with another guy and a girl. That guy was SO hot. When she got a chance to talk to him later she had just clammed up and looked stupid. It didn't matter though. The tall, curvy thing he was with had her claws deep into him. No way he was breaking free. A moment after he walked away laughing, Pedro was at her side. She heard his voice before she saw him.

"He's not worth your attention anyway. Just a mama's boy. What you need is a real man."

"Oh, and you think you're the kind of man I need, I bet." She dipped her *head down and tipped it sideways to look up at him through her extended eyelashes. Making herself appear smaller and more vulnerable had always drawn guys in. They couldn't resist. But to her astonishment, Pedro laughed at her.*

"Oh, ho! So you've got all the moves. Planning to reel me in like some poor unsuspecting fish and then chew me up and leave me hangin. No, thank you. Not interested." And he walked away, pausing to flirt with every girl *along the way*

She snapped back to the present when she heard Pedro's voice saying, "Annabelle, oh Annabelle, how you steal my heart away sitting there with the sunshine dancing off your golden hair." *I should've let him walk away!* Annabelle hated the sarcastic note in his voice, but she responded the way she always had.

"Pedro! Stop it. You're making me blush." She tipped her head and fluttered her lashes up at him. Then she stood up straight and pressed her body into his, kissing him passionately. *Might as well enjoy the only good parts of him.*

When they came up for air, Pedro asked her, "What brings you to the river today?"

She never told Pedro about the end of her story. He didn't know how she would die. And since his IQ was lower than a slug's, she doubted he had ever read his own story to the end. She doubted he knew she was close to death. And she wasn't about to tell him now. He didn't deserve to know.

"Planning," she replied curtly. "I got kicked out of the governor's house right before the final score." That still burned her butt. Why hadn't she waited one more day? *Oh, right, the book.*

Pedro's face darkened. He was angry, and she really couldn't blame him—this time. He had the buyer all lined up. Not coming through with that painting wasn't good for his rep. Hers either. But she was always behind the scenes. He was the one with contacts to keep happy.

"Listen. I couldn't do anything about it. You know that."

"Annabelle, I'm getting sick of you not coming through for me. It's like you like getting caught! How could you possibly have screwed up such a simple operation!?! I gift-wrapped that one for you. It was fool-proof!" He shoved her back down into her seat and cussed. Then he picked up a large stone and threw it as hard as he could into the water. Annabelle stared at the ripples it created and kept back the tears by sheer willpower. She wouldn't let him see her cry.

"Ok, so what's the next plan? It had better be good." Pedro turned back toward her and compelled her to look at him.

"I don't have one yet. But, I was thinking…"

"I was thinking about those office buildings on the other side of the river." She breathed the words out as quickly as she could. It was a stupid idea. How could she ever sell it to Pedro? *Dammit!* She shouldn't have said a word to him. Now, she had to make a secondary plan for once she got across.

Pedro's head jerked up and he looked across the river wide-eyed like he had never seen the other side before. She could see the wheels turning in his head, and then the cunning look of greed replaced the anger of moments before.

"Every single one of those offices has artwork equal to the governor's house. Why didn't we ever try this before?"

"Because, idiot, NO ONE crosses the river." She didn't have to remind him of that. It was common knowledge that Canree Nu East was off-limits to anyone from the West. She didn't even know why the bridge existed except for the deliveries that went out once a month. All the Future Books for the island were created in Canree Nu

West and went directly to the Writer. He wrote the stories out for Canree Nu West. Annabelle didn't know what he did with the ones for the East Island. But then he sent them out across the bridge in a large truck. At that thought, a lopsided grin grew across her face. Pedro noticed instantly.

"Tell me. How are you going to get across?"

"The truck."

CHAPTER 3

Chapter 6—Day 2

You wake up with a pounding headache. The light through your closed eyes is too much to handle, so you throw your sleeping bag up over your head and groan. You start thinking back over the day before when you and Pedro discussed how to make the plan work and where the best marks would be. You worked for hours, and as the sun went down, Pedro pulled out the alcohol.

Annabelle groaned again. Why did she do that!? Why did she always do that? She remembered the first hangover—it was the day after she met Pedro. That day, she watched him flirting with all the girls and knew she had to have him. She had "accidentally" bumped into him near the drinks. He gave her her first drink, and it was all downhill from there. When she got back to the Caretaker's house late that night— well, really early the next morning—every room was dark. She knew Caretaker would be awake in her bed until she knew she was home safe, and Protector would be watching out the window for her.

The next morning had been murder, trying to convince both her Protector and her Caretaker that she was just feeling a little ill. It wasn't an easy sell; she never got sick. But they didn't have any reason not to believe her at that point. She did overhear them having a serious conversation in the next room later that day. Protector wasn't buying it, but she could tell Caretaker really wanted to. Caretaker convinced her Protector to wait it out and see where things go from there. That was when Annabelle decided to get really good at lying. She didn't tell Caretaker and Protector about Pedro that day or the next. It was a full month of sneaking out and partying and hiding the effects before she let them know she met a guy.

Thinking back to that first big lie, she knew it was where everything started breaking down. As the months and years passed, Caretaker grew… sad. She started looking older more often. The effects of going away with her book didn't last as long. Annabelle's Protector grew distant. She started seeing him more across the street than she did at home. More than once, she thought he might've been the person who pulled her out of harm's way. But Protector never talked about it. He never talked much about anything. The more she lied, the fewer questions he asked. He just shook his head and looked *disappointed*. She hated that look.

Annabelle rolled over and as she did, her face encountered something crinkly that rustled. She opened one eye and looked at it. *Another envelope.* Still under the sleeping bag she excitedly pulled the envelope open. The last envelope had given her a *great* idea. Maybe this one would help with the plan. She looked at the faint writing and could barely make it out.

"You can be free. Tell the tru…"

The end faded off into oblivion. Weird.
Ugh! Tell the truth. Tell the truth. Tell the truth. I'm already free!! I can

do whatever I like! And like I would ever be free if I told the truth. I'd get thrown into prison instantly. Annabelle grimaced at the thought of her Caretaker saying almost the same thing.

"The truth will set you free, Annabelle."

What did she know, anyway? She had no idea how bad the truth really was. Annabelle tossed the newest message into the corner of her box. She had work to do, and none of it involved the truth. She turned her mind to the next job and the truck she needed. It was kept behind the outer court of the Keeper. The truck and the driver's uniform were both a very peculiar shade of green. She needed to know what it was in order to duplicate the uniform. She would also need to recreate the Keeper's seal, embroidered on the left front pocket of the shirt. For just a second, she hesitated. Going through with this plan meant kidnapping and holding one of the drivers hostage while she took his place and went across the bridge. She had never done anything like that before, but there really wasn't another way. They had looked at every angle. Anyway, it wouldn't be her holding the driver hostage. It would be Pedro. He didn't care at all about taking the next step up in crime.

He was capable of murder.

The scene she had pictured a thousand times flashed through her mind. Her last day to live. A knife in her hand and Pedro standing in front of her. Annabelle shuddered. She *had* to change her story. This *had* to work. But the more she was determined to see this through and change her story, the more she realized she was pushing the story forward to its inevitable conclusion. She shook off the visions of the future. *Just do what you have to for today!*

You exit your box, too eager to bother with breakfast today. You must get to the outer court of the Keeper and somehow figure out when the next shipment of Future Books goes across to Canree Nu East. That's where the whole plan breaks down in your head. If you can't figure that out, you're never going to get across the bridge.

Annabelle tossed her bag over her shoulder and started out. A few blocks later, something caught her eye down by one of the cafes. It was a fluttering of some fabric—lighter than air. She looked closer and saw the Messenger was there, hovering near a gorgeous young black woman who was crying over her tea. The Messenger took the hand of a tall, slender young man in a green uniform and drew him near the young woman. It looked like the Messenger was talking to him while gesturing to the young woman. Annabelle had never seen so many words come out of the Messenger at one time. Then the Messenger moved on to another person, leaving the uniformed man to talk with the young woman. A flash of light across his left pocket revealed he was one of the drivers who took the Future Books across the bridge. She couldn't believe her luck! All she had to do was get close to him, and she could copy the seal. She felt around the bottom of her bag, looking for some coins to buy tea. She had barely enough to cover a cup.

As she walked past the tall man and crying woman, she overheard him reciting something—it sounded almost like poetry but she was certain there was nothing romantic going on there. The young man's face was animated and alive as he spoke the ancient words. Whatever it was, it meant something to him. And to the woman. Her tears stopped flowing as she listened. Annabelle found a table next to them and sat down. The young woman immediately stood up and walked over to her.

"Welcome to Rosa's Cafe! I'm Rosa, what can I get for you today?" She offered a brilliant smile and then sniffed.

"Oh, I'm sorry to interrupt. I'd really like an herbal tea, please."

"Certainly, I'll bring you some choices and hot water. Just a moment!"

Annabelle thanked Rosa as she scurried off, bumping into a chair and the doorjamb as she went. Then Annabelle stole a glance at the young man in green, but he was looking right at her. His eyes were a clear blue like the sky on a summer afternoon. She didn't like the way he looked right through her; it reminded her of Protector. She quickly looked down at the tiny flowers on the table. Rosa was back only moments later with a steaming teapot. The cup and saucer were a delicate pink with tiny roses around the edges. Rosa had brought several different kinds of tea as well as some croissants. Annabelle blushed.

"Oh, um, well actually, I just... I just have money for the tea."

Rosa smiled at her, "I thought as much! The croissants are a gift. Enjoy them."

Annabelle smiled back automatically and then turned her gaze down to the inviting display. "Thank you." She couldn't remember the last time she thanked someone. She couldn't remember the last time someone had done something nice for her. For a second, she wondered what the angle was, but looking back at Rosa as she sat once again, she couldn't see anything fake about her. Annabelle picked up a lemon tea and transferred the bag to the teapot. She suddenly remembered she hadn't eaten breakfast as her tummy grumbled at her. She stuffed the first croissant into her mouth, thinking *Thank you, Keeper, for Rosa.* The thought took her by surprise. Caretaker taught her that everything good came from the Keeper and that she needed to thank him for them. But she hadn't done anything like that in all the years since she left Caretaker's house. She wondered why she thought of that today. *Oh well.* Annabelle mentally shrugged.

Next to her, the young man picked up the story he was telling Rosa. From what Annabelle could hear it was a story filled with drama and tension. She almost got drawn into the story and forgot her mission. *The seal.* The young man's back was to her so there was no way to see what it was unless she somehow got his attention. But she really didn't *want* his attention either. Those understanding blue eyes made her uncomfortable! She looked over the table in front of her. All she really had to work with was a vase with small flowers and her tea. He looked like a gentleman, and he was in the service of the Keeper. If she *spilled* her tea, he was practically duty-bound to help her clean it up. She could see the seal up close and personal while he sopped up the spilled tea. But she was still hungry, so she stuffed the second croissant into her mouth, taking time to notice how light and fluffy it was.

You swallow the final bit of flaky goodness and take a sip of tea. The tea burns your top lip and your tongue just a little bit. You think you'd better wait until it won't burn your legs, so you sit back and look around. The street is actually kind of sweet. Little pink flowers poke out of the sidewalk, giving the whole place a facelift. The buildings are still browning and older, but the flowers take away from the feeling of despair that most of Canree Nu West portrays. You notice the flowers on the table match the ones in the cracks of the sidewalk. That must be where Rosa gets them. A tiny, furry creature darts out from next to the building and scoops up some crumbs left by a previous customer. It scurries back to where it came from.

Annabelle fingered the tiny pink flowers in the vase at her table. It was soft and bright. She couldn't help but notice the ones in the sidewalk cracks to match it. Rosa had done her best to brighten up the dim storefront that served as a cafe. Bright curtains reflected the sunlight through the perfectly clean windows. Annabelle turned her attention to the crumbs on the ground next to her, waiting for the little creature to appear. But out of the corner of her eye, the fluttering robes of the Messenger moved past, and she turned to look. The Messenger was leaning over the young man and whispering something to him. He nodded twice, then said, "Ok, I'll be there soon." The messenger moved on down the road. Rosa looked to the young man with bright eyes.

"Will you come back sometime? I want to hear more of the story."

Annabelle realized with a shock she had to move quickly before the young man took his leave. She knocked over her teacup and sent the scalding tea cascading over the side of the table and to the ground. As she suspected he would, the young man jumped up and grabbed a napkin all in one smooth motion, kneeling next to her table to sop up the mess. He looked up at her with a grin.

"Here, let me help with that," he said. His eyes looked straight into hers knowingly before he returned his attention to the mess. Rosa ran to the back of the shop to get more towels and more tea.

Annabelle jumped on her chance, looking at the intricate design. It was embroidered with golden thread. The center held the face of a lion with a crown. On top of the crown, there was a crimson heart. All around the face, there was a thorny vine wound in circles. It would be easy enough to get some thread and make her own! Victory!

When Rosa returned, the young man had already contained the mess. He stood and deposited the soiled napkins on the tray she held out to him. He smiled at her and said, "Chin up, sister! You may never know the good you've already done today. I'll be back soon to finish the story." Rosa spontaneously hugged him, and he laughed, a deep, rich laugh of pure joy. He hugged her back, picking her up a little before patting her back and moving down the street. His long legs gave him kind of a loping canter as he quickly went off to catch up with the Messenger. Rosa placed a new teacup and teabag on the table and went to ask another customer if they needed anything else. Annabelle drank another cup of tea before continuing her trip to the Keeper's outer court.

When you reach the garden next to the outer court, you look around and realize that by pulling out your notebook and pencil, you can camouflage yourself as a student. They are all over the garden, posing up a storm, thinking their deep thoughts and jotting down notes, or reading thick books of island history. You find a low stone wall that's perfect for sitting on. It's near the back with a view of the truck and close enough to hear any workers who may come through.

Annabelle scanned the back of the garden and quickly found the stone wall the Future Book mentioned. She settled herself on it and dug out her notebook and pencil, throwing on her sweatshirt with the hood up over her head. She could almost lean her head back on the wall behind her and fall asleep, dreaming of the tea and croissants she just consumed. She closed her eyes, smiled, and sighed the happiest sigh in history. A sudden metallic noise pulled her back into the present and her eyes flew open, noting a tall, thin man who had just closed an iron gate with a bang. The gate had a strange symbol at the top of it. He was staring straight at her with a serious look, but his hazel eyes twinkled, and the wind-tossed his sandy brown curls around. He lifted one hand to his hat in a gesture of greeting, and Annabelle offered back an involuntary "Hi." Only then did it register that he was wearing the same green uniform as the other young man. *I could use another look at that seal.* The young man started walking toward her, and as he got close, she looked intently at the seal embroidered on his chest pocket. To her surprise, it didn't look the same as the other man's. The other one had a lion, but this one had an eagle with wings spread wide and a crimson eye. The same twisted, spiny vine was wound in a circle around it. Perplexed, she dropped her attention to her open notebook. *What do I do now?*

"It's a beautiful morning, isn't it, miss?"

His voice startled her. "Uh, uh, yes. Beautiful. I just love coming here to study."

He nodded in agreement. "Yeah, a lot of students come around here. They like the gardens and being close to the Keeper. There's a whole lotta peace around here."

Peace. Is that what this feeling is?

He continued in his slow, soothing tone, "Yeah, no place better than the Keeper's court. There's so much beauty here. Myself, I like the statues." He pointed to four separate statues in the corners of the garden. Annabelle hadn't noticed them before. They were intricately carved wooden statues as tall as the trees around them. She gasped as she saw first a lion and then an eagle. The other two looked like a person and a cow.

"Well, hope your day is a good one. I've gotta get back to work. Nice meeting you....?"

"Annabelle," she replied when she realized he was looking for her to fill in the blank.

"Annabelle," he echoed with a kind but knowing look in his eye. "Nice to meet you, Annabelle. I'm the Watcher." He made a motion like he was about to move on. She grabbed his sleeve, and he paused, looking down at her quizzically.

"Um, Can I ask you something, Watcher? I saw another young man earlier today wearing a uniform like you, but his shirt had a lion on it. Who was he? And why do you have different seals?"

The Watcher smiled at her. "That's my brother. He's the Comforter. And I guess because we do different things." And with a shrug and a wave, he was gone.

Annabelle looked down at her notebook and sketched both the lion and the eagle. She looked over at the statues of the cow and the man and wondered if there were people out there with those pictures in golden seals. To be safe, she decided to draw them as well. She would decide later which one to copy for her fake uniform.

Someone walked toward the iron gate the Watcher had come out of. Annabelle watched intently as they raised their hand, and the gate clicked open. She looked down at her own palm and wondered if the strange white mark would also open it. But she didn't dare try with so many people around. Instead, she picked up her bag and headed back toward the shopping district to find some gold and crimson thread.

CHAPTER 4

Chapter 6—Day 3, in the afternoon

You stop and wipe the sweat from your forehead. The mornings are still cool, but the afternoons are getting warmer. Taking a quick drink of water from a nearby fountain, you carry on your way down to the Keeper's garden again. Irritated that you'd forgotten all about finding out the schedule for the next Future Book delivery, and with your head buried in your notebook, you don't notice the older man coming toward you on the sidewalk, and you almost knock him over.

Annabelle jerked her head up as she remembered the next happening from the book but she was too late. Her shoulder collided with an older gentleman's and he nearly lost his footing. Kicking herself and hating the book, she kept walking past him as fast as she could. Apologizing wasn't her thing. *Keep your head on, Annabelle. You've got one job. Find you way across the bridge so you can change your story!* She hoped her spot from yesterday was open. It had turned out to be the greatest spot ever when that young Keeper's worker had stopped to chat. Annabelle had decided to embroider the cow's head on her fake uniform and hope against hope it would pass.

You round the corner and see that your spot is taken today. You look for another place close to the gate and the truck but don't see one close enough to hear any conversation. But there is a picnic table close enough to see the comings and goings around the truck. Maybe you would find a clue in that. So you sit at the table, once again pulling out your notebook and pencil. Your cow drawing could use some work anyway.

Annabelle started over with her sketch of the cow's head. Where she sat, there was a perfect view of the cow statue, and today, she wasn't in a hurry. She took her time studying the angles and restarted several times, all the while watching the area near the truck. The whole garden felt sleepy today—the muggy air had everyone moving slowly. And there was no movement near the truck for over an hour. *Maybe they're all on lunch break.*

You notice two people walking over to the gate. One of them, an older woman, lifts her hand, and the gate clicks open. She has her arm around the younger man, who seems to be limping. They go in together, and the gate slides shut behind them. As it closes, something near the top shoots a flash of reflected sunlight past your eyes. You blink against the glare. Looking over to the low stone wall, you realize the person who sat there has moved on, so you gather up your things and take a better position for watching and listening. A squirrel that had been dashing about the garden scurries up the tree and scolds you loudly when you start over to the wall.

Annabelle spotted the squirrel and laughed. He was a small gray squirrel with a very bushy tail that almost pulled him off balance as he ran. He reached the tree when she got to the wall. She sat down and waited to be scolded, but she didn't hear anything but the rustling of some leaves further up. *Weird. Where did he go?* She sat back against the tree and looked up through the branches. There, perched happily on a thin branch, was the squirrel. He was busy nibbling on an acorn. *Did I... Did I remember that wrong? Maybe the squirrel scolds me on a different day.* Annabelle was unsettled. She couldn't remember getting anything from the Future Book mixed up before. Before she could ponder it further, the woman and young man walked out of the gate. He was laughing and running ahead of her, then he turned and rushed back to sweep her up in a hug. Annabelle just stared, wondering if she imagined the limp earlier. *What is behind that gate?*

You don't have to wait long for the next person to enter the gate. This time, it's an older man. You recognize the man you ran into on your way to the garden. He can barely lift his arm or spread his hand, but when he tries, you hear the same click, and the gate swings open. For just a second, you think about the old man and wonder about his story. What mark did he have? What do the marks mean anyway? You trace the twisted white mark on your palm out of habit. You sit back against the tree to wait for him to come out. The garden isn't that active today; maybe when he leaves, there will be an opening for you to try to get in.

Annabelle tipped her head back and closed her eyes, resting a moment while she waited for the old man to come out. A slight breeze stirred in the garden. The sound of it rustling through the leaves and the sunlight dancing through the branches onto her face enhanced the feeling of deep peace in the garden, and soon, Annabelle was nodding off. As she drifted off to sleep, she started dreaming.

Annabelle stood up and headed for the statue of the cow. At the base was a gate just like the one she had been watching. She lifted up her arm and opened her hand. The gate swung open silently, and she walked through the statue. Behind it was a dense forest with a single path. She followed the narrow, dimly lit path back through the forest. As she made her way back, she saw an older woman carrying a heavy load. When she got close, she recognized her Caretaker, but she was much older than Annabelle remembered, and she was crying. Annabelle gently took the Caretaker's load from her, then led her to a fallen tree where she could rest. Without any words being spoken, Annabelle understood that she was to bring the load to the end of the path. She continued on her way, noticing another person in the distance. As she got closer, the person loomed larger and larger, and she realized it was her Protector. He had an oversized machete, and he was clearing the path ahead of her. Looking back, the narrow path was cleared and easy to walk. Turning and looking ahead, Annabelle saw the path was overgrown and difficult to get through. Tears poured down the Protector's face. Annabelle watched him swing the machete and clear the path for a moment. Every movement seemed to be painful for him, and she noticed something she had never seen before. He was covered in wounds in various stages of healing. Some larger, some smaller, and some wide open and fresh. She touched his shoulder, and he stopped swinging. She held out her hand, and he placed the machete in it. It had shrunk to a size she could wield. She started swinging and clearing her own path, leaving her Protector standing behind her. Far ahead of her, she saw another gate, and she knew that was her goal.

A loud clang startled Annabelle out of her dreams. She blinked and realized that she was back in the Keeper's garden. The clouds had moved in and covered the sun. Looking around she saw the garden was empty except for one man who was walking away. He was tall and moved purposely with a straight back and firm gait. Annabelle shook her head to clear the cobwebs. How long had she been asleep? The older man must've already left and the handsome younger guy had come while she slept. The dream left her disoriented and unsure of her next step, so Annabelle started thinking through what the Future book said about today. She just... couldn't remember anything about a nap.

When the younger man walks away, you jump up and move to the gate. Now's your chance to see what's back there. Maybe it will explain the mark on your hand. Or maybe, and this would be even better, the schedule of Future Book deliveries will be somewhere behind that gate. When you get close, you see that the bright, reflective marker on the top of the door has each of the four creatures from the statues in the garden woven around each other. You mimic the waving motion you had seen, stretching your arm up and opening your palm toward the marker, and... nothing happens. No creak, no clink of opening locks. Nothing. You take a step back and approach again. You lift up your arm and open your hand, waving it back and forth slowly, but again, nothing happens. Looking around to make sure the garden is still clear, you examine the lock and bolt across the gate. It's like nothing you've ever seen before. The works are so intricately interwoven that they look like one continual piece. You decide it's too complicated to pick the lock and head back to your wall and tree, stymied.

Annabelle sat down again, frustrated. She was no closer to fulfilling her plan than she was at the beginning of the day, and she didn't know what to do next. She only had nine days left before her death. Time was short, and instead of getting anything done, she had fallen asleep in the garden! She grabbed her backpack and roughly shoved everything back into it. No use in sticking around here any longer. Nobody was here, and nothing was happening. She couldn't get into the gate. There was no sign of the uniformed young men. Images from her dream kept popping up in her head, stirring something uncomfortable inside she hadn't acknowledged in years. She hadn't seen or talked to her Caretaker or Protector since the day she walked out. They never understood her. They never cared. They thought she *wanted* to trick them, to lie to them, and only show them a fake version of who she was. She tried to show them her Future Book, but they wouldn't open it. They kept saying she had a choice when she had NO choice. They couldn't see how stuck she was in this endless cycle of lies and exposure.

"All we want from you is the truth." She could hear Caretaker's voice ringing through her head. *Why* did they want the one thing she couldn't give them? Couldn't they be happy with the gifts and the cards and letters that said she loved them? Then, at the end, there was one day where she just couldn't take it anymore, and she walked out the door. She could still see Protector's ashen face as he asked her not to let something so small come between them.

Annabelle threw her backpack over her shoulder impatiently. Once the door to memories of Caretaker and Protector was opened, it was hard to close it again against the flood of emotions that poured out, but she didn't have time for that today. Or any day. It hurt too much to think about it all. She stood to her feet and started off through the garden to the street. Tears she didn't ask for muddied her vision, and she found herself plowing into another person on the sidewalk. She pushed past, utterly frustrated with herself for getting caught up in the past again. She had successfully pushed away every memory for years now. Maybe it was the looming presence of death that was making her emotional and weak. She stormed through the city, not paying attention to where she was going as she tried to shove the memories back behind the door. The tunnel vision caused by all this finally diminished, and she noticed tiny pink flowers on the sidewalk. She looked up and realized she had walked herself all the way back to Rosa's Cafe.

She flipped her backpack to the front and reached around the bottom of it, feeling for any loose coins she may have left. She once again found just enough for a cup of tea and plopped herself next to the white table dropping her backpack in a second chair. The street and the storefront were quiet. She tried to look in through the plate glass window but the reflection kept her from seeing inside. Were they even open?

You reluctantly stand up and go to the door, where you see a small sign indicating the Cafe is closed. You don't know why you're so depressed by that news since you didn't even intend to go there in the first place. You don't want to go to the river because Pedro may be there, and he's the last thing you want to deal with when you feel like this. You try and fail to come up with another place to go, slowly realizing that Pedro and the river are all you have. You've pushed every other person out of your life. You lied to every friend—and were found out one too many times. They all left, angry. You turn around and head for the market to steal something to eat. Then you'll head to the river.

Normally, realizing she was all alone in the world except for her Companion, who was more of a headache than anything else, would make her angry. But today, the dream in the garden had sapped the life out of her, and she dragged herself through finding something to eat. When she got to the river, Pedro was already there and sitting in her chair. The spark of irritation she felt let her know the anger wasn't gone, just buried.

"Get out of my chair," she snapped at him.

"Hello to you, too, beautiful." In his voice, the beautiful sounded snide. But he did get out of her chair. She collapsed into it and started eating the loaf of bread and hunk of cheese she had managed to snatch from one of the street vendors. Pedro reached into her crevice and pulled out the green uniform she had stashed there yesterday. "So, I see you're making progress on the plan. I've talked to several of my buyers and they're all *very* interested in the product you will come up with. What day can I tell them you'll have it for them?"

Annabelle rolled her eyes at him and kept eating. She knew from her Future Book that tonight would end with an argument, but she wanted to put it off as long as she could—until she was finished eating, at least. Pedro grabbed the bread out of her hand, took a bite, and threw the rest into the river. "Are you gonna answer me or what?" He punctuated his feelings by calling her a foul name. Annabelle glared at him. The desire to cry *again* was overwhelming, but she couldn't cry in front of him, so she fanned the spark of irritation into a flame of rage. She pulled out her knife and used it to slice her next hunk of cheese, deliberately ignoring Pedro as he practically breathed fire in front of her. The one thing he couldn't stand was being ignored. If you tried to fight him with words, he always won, piling insults on top of stinging barbs. He always knew just where to strike. And she couldn't even dream of being his equal physically. Ignoring him was her best weapon. She knew the knife would send her message loud and clear—don't mess with me today.

Pedro stared at her for a full thirty seconds, then moved away. He grabbed a discarded glass bottle and threw it full force at the bridge supports. It shattered. Annabelle glanced at it as the pieces fell into the river, then moved her attention back to carefully slicing her cheese. She drew it out, deliberately and slowly taking each bite. When she was finally finished she stood and walked over to where Pedro fumed. She yanked the uniform out of his grasp and put it back into its hiding spot. Then she faced him again with her knife still in her hand.

"Where do you get off, coming into MY space, using MY chair, and then demanding answers about MY operation?!? I'll give you the information you need *when* you need it and not before! You can't demand *anything* from me."

"Like hell, I can't. You're the one who screwed up the *entire* con in the governor's house. You know how badly you screwed up that one and lost me one of my best clients. One of *your* best clients! You blew the biggest deal in one stupid move, just like you always do. I don't know why I even keep working with you."

"You know why, you idiot. The Future Books. If it weren't for them, I'd have dumped you a long time ago."

"That's the other way around, and you know it. You couldn't keep a buyer if your life depended on it. I'm the only reason you've made any money at your stupid cons. Without me, you'd just be making enough money to buy lunch."

"That's all I'm doing anyway," she screamed at him. "I will never get off this stupid island!" She dropped the knife and fell to her knees. "Just leave me alone. Go away."

Annabelle heard Pedro scramble up the embankment and shuffle down the road. Only when she was sure he was gone did she let the tears flow again. She looked through tear-filled eyes at the ground where her knife fell. It looked a lot like the day she dies—a day that was still in the future but played through her mind like a memory. She looked around from the same spot as the final chapter in her book and crumpled into a crying heap.

CHAPTER 5

Chapter 6—Day 4

You wake up slowly with a cool breeze blowing over you. You're a little groggy and stiff and very confused. You open your eyes and realize it's dark out. Shivering, you notice you're still in the same place you sank to your knees the evening before. You groan and roll over onto your back and stretch.

𝒜 nnabelle looked up at the stars, unsure of what to do next. It was hours until dawn, but remembering the argument the night before left her brain buzzing. Even if she were warm enough, she wouldn't be able to sleep again. She got up, grabbed her hoodie out of her bag, and put it on. She contemplated making a try for the locked gate but quickly dismissed the idea. That lock was too complicated. Thinking she may find another entrance, she decided to head toward the Keeper's garden anyway. No one would be there this time of night, and the moon was full and giving off plenty of light. She could explore everything freely. She lifted her bag over her shoulder and started toward the middle of the city.

You head for the garden by the light of the moon. The cool breeze clears your mind, and the walk feels good. You pick up the pace and pass Rosa's Cafe. Seeing the sign reminds you of the delicious croissants of the other morning. You've still got enough change for tea; maybe when it opens, you'll head there for breakfast. There's no one in sight all the way to the garden, but as you enter, you see a shadowy figure by the gate. A single cloud covers the moon. The shape seems familiar but you don't dare get closer right now. You wait near the entrance, watching while they lift their hand and walk through the gate. You hear the clank as it closes behind them.

The Keeper's Garden lay to the east of the courtyard. The brick wall of the court was two stories tall, broken up only by the foliage creeping up the sides. At the top, there were a couple of feet of colored glass. Annabelle thought briefly that it's what must give the inner area it's dim, mysterious lighting. As she followed the wall to the south, there was the gate it seemed everyone could get in except her. Behind it was a flight of stairs down below the wall and then a door. But there was no way to access that door from where she was. The gate was the only way. She kept moving around the corner of the building to the back alley where the truck was parked. Storage buildings lined the opposite side of the alley. She glanced over at them and then dismissed them quickly. The locks on them were simple to pick, so there couldn't be anything truly valuable to her in those buildings. Turning her attention to the court wall, she saw it looked just like the one facing the garden. It was too tall to scale, with colored glass all along the top.

Suddenly, the moon peeks out from behind its cloud, revealing a single metal door. That's your chance! You move quickly through the alley to the door. It's not a simple lock, but it isn't impossible like the one on the gate. Carefully checking both directions down the alley, you lift your backpack off your shoulder and set it on the ground. You unzip the front pocket and pull out several thin metal tools. You think to yourself that at least Pedro had been good for something.

Pedro was always more comfortable picking locks than she was, but a couple of the cons she ran required creative entry into locked places that Pedro couldn't help her with. She crouched near the door, making herself as small as she could, and started working on the lock. It was pretty still in the city, but she didn't want the odd person walking past to make her and sound an alarm. She wondered briefly about the Keeper. His one eye focused on her the day she tore out the page that sometimes popped up in her dreams. She felt like he could see her no matter where she was. She shuddered at the thought and then returned her focus to the lock. This was taking too long.

You're so focused on your work that you don't register the sound of the gate clanging shut.

The next words from her Future Book flashed across her eyes. *Oh no! Did I miss that already? Is someone coming this way?* Annabelle grabbed her bag and bolted for the space between two of the storage units across the street. She tried to remember what came next—*am I caught again?* But the words seemed blurry and far away. She shook her head as if to clear it. From around the corner, she heard the muffled clank of the gate. *What! No. That's not right.* Annabelle's heart rate skyrocketed. She could feel the familiar sweep of adrenaline through her body. The storage wall in front of her face became crystal clear while everything else grew blurry and dark. Her heart pounded out of her chest. She heard footsteps in the alley, but it was like they were miles away. She couldn't regain control of her senses. It was like she was looking at someone else's life.

The humming she heard from the person walking through the alley was familiar. It was an old song she knew she had heard before, but it was more than that. The voice was familiar. The footsteps marked out a rhythm she had heard a million times before. Her breath released, and her mind settled back into itself. The tune washed over her and slowed her heart rate until she felt like herself again. Only then did she piece together the sensations into one complete picture. *Caretaker*. What were the chances of her walking down this particular street in the middle of the night? As the calm washed over her body, the writing in her mind became clear once again.

> Caretaker passes the spot where you're hiding close
> enough for you to reach out and touch her, and for a
> brief moment, you almost want to. Instead, you sink
> back into the shadows, moving as stealthily and slowly as
> you can. The moon shines on Caretaker's face and you see
> she's looking young— maybe younger than she ever looked
> when you were with her. With a sudden realization, you
> connect that she was the figure in the garden that was
> headed to the gate. Caretaker knew the secret of opening
> the gate. You tuck the knowledge away for future use.
> Caretaker turns the corner and the humming grows faint.
> The spell the tune wove over you fades, and with it, all
> of the lighter feelings. You feel the familiar hardness
> return and settle around your heart. You snatch up your
> backpack angrily and return to the metal door, more deter-
> mined than ever to get inside. You set to work on the lock

one more time. You feel a new sense of urgency in the work. You're so focused on your work that you don't register the sound of the gate clanging shut.

Annabelle jerked her head up, utterly confused, as she went back in her memory and pulled out the sound of the gate slamming shut again moments ago. She grabbed her bag and ran away from the garden and the court. The repeated line in the Future Book, mixed with the time of being unable to remember what came next, all had her head feeling scrambled. And what on earth was behind that gate that people would be going in there all hours of the night? Nowhere in Canree Nu was that busy that late. Annabelle headed back to her box as quickly as she could. It was too early to do anything else, and she wasn't about to risk getting caught at that door. Two brushes with being discovered were two too many for her. And if she somehow couldn't remember again what happened next, her chances of getting caught skyrocketed. When she got back to her box, she settled in, heaved a sigh, and immediately fell asleep.

You open your eyes. Clouds cover the sun but it still brightens the sky enough to wake you up. The events of the night before run through your mind. Sleep granted clarity. In order to get into the gate, you have to get Caretaker to bring you with her, just like the old woman who brought the young man. The only trouble is, you haven't been in contact with Caretaker in years. There's a whisper at the side of your box, and an envelope flutters in.

To move forward, you must go back. The truth will set yo....

Just like the last one, the letters faded out. But she was sure of what the unreadable letters would have said. The truth will set you free. She tore the envelope and the card in two. She *would* go backward to go forward. But there would be no truth involved. She needed to figure out a really good story for why she was suddenly back and why she needed to get into the gate. Her stomach rumbled, and she knew she wouldn't get anywhere on an empty stomach. With memories of Rosa's tea and croissants floating in her mind, she grabbed a couple of dollars from her jar. She threw some dry shampoo into her hair, switched to a cleaner sun dress, and headed out to Rosa's Cafe. The tea and pastries called to her, but deep down, she knew it was more than that. It was Rosa herself. She was the first person to treat her with genuine kindness in a long, long time.

You get to the Cafe and settle into a chair with your backpack dropped next to you. It's early yet, so the little pink flowers in the sidewalk are barely opening up. The street is starting to wake up, with people getting in their cars and on bikes and heading to work. You keep your head down and your eyes focused on the small vase in the middle of the table. A bell on the door lets you know Rosa is headed your way. You look up and she gives you a smile. There are streaks through her makeup that show she has been crying, but she still manages to look pleased to see you. You stumble through a hello and give your order. She disappears inside.

Annabelle paid for tea *and* croissants this time. She watched Rosa head back into the cafe to get them. Rosa had painted a new sign in the past couple of days. It had tiny pink flowers around the edges and brightened up the front of the shop. Annabelle had intended to work out her plan for getting Caretaker to get her into the gate, but sitting there, she couldn't. She would have to go back to her chair by the river to figure that out. For the moment, she let herself enjoy the narrow street and the small pink flowers. Rosa reappeared with her tea and croissants. Annabelle noticed her makeup had been repaired in the brief time she was inside. She picked up the delicate tea cup and inhaled the earthy scent. The smell triggered a memory from her first days with Caretaker and Protector. She was new and scared. Nothing in her early life prepared her to be under authority like that. She spent most of her time listening around corners and stealing food from the cupboards. They fed her plenty of food, but almost every day, she found herself lurking in the kitchen, waiting for an opportunity. She couldn't explain it, but stealing food made her feel more alive and more powerful. And definitely more in control. The Protector caught her that day as she snuck out of the kitchen with a slice of cheese and an apple.

Protector was angry, and she was terrified. It was the first time she had been caught in the act, and she didn't know what the large man would do. He yelled at her and told her she didn't need to steal any food. All she *needed* to do was ask if she was hungry. How could she explain she wasn't even really hungry? She just needed to steal it. Listening to Protector talk about truth and trust, she found herself growing more and more angry. She would take the food whenever needed, and she didn't care what they said. Inwardly, she seethed. Outwardly, she cried, and with wide eyes staring straight into Protector's, she said she would never steal again.

She stole twice more that day—first a snack cake and then some grapes—just to find herself again. She didn't care that the Keeper had brought her to the Caretaker and Protector. She didn't care that they were supposed to take care of her, and she was supposed to listen to them. She just wanted her life in the box back, where food was sometimes given to her, but she did everything else herself. She came and went as she pleased and no one told her what to do. She had watched the other kids in their uniforms doing their homework and chores and thought she would hate that life. When the Keeper moved her to the Caretaker and Protector, she found out she was right. She did hate that life. More than anything, she hated being told what to do

Later that same day, in between stealing the cake and stealing the grapes, Protector had made her a cup of tea. That was the smell that triggered the memory. All the lecturing and raised voices were done, and he was trying to understand what was wrong. She led him down a tale so twisted and embellished that he eventually gave up looking for the truth. The truth was, she didn't know why she stole it. She didn't know what was wrong with her. But she couldn't tell him that truth. In her mind, he needed something more if he was going to believe her. She learned that day that she could weave a story and be believed. She needed that skill today to get Caretaker to do what she needed. Suddenly impatient with being in the tiny Cafe, she grabbed the croissants and stood to go.

"Is everything ok?" Rosa's voice broke into her memories. Annabelle had forgotten all about her as she walked through the past.

"What? Uh, yes. Yes, everything was great."

"But are you ok?" Rosa asked her with a look of genuine concern. She held up an envelope. "The messenger left this while you were staring off into nowhere."

Annabelle's eyes widened as she took the note from Rosa. She opened it and inside were only four words. The last one faded to nothing.

This is your cha...

Her chance to what? She wished the messenger left better clues. She looked up and noticed Rosa was still looking at her expectantly. Oh, she had asked her something.

"Um, yes, I'm ok."

"Are you sure? You looked lost in thought, and then you suddenly put down your tea without drinking a sip! I can put that in a to-go cup if you like." Rosa motioned to the tea while she spoke.

"Oh. Um, yes, thank you. I would like that. Thank you."

Rosa moved quickly, but when she tried to pour the tea into the new cup, she spilled most of it on the table. She laughed so loudly that Annabelle couldn't help but join in. The sound surprised her—she hadn't laughed just to laugh at any point in her memory. Every laugh was planned for maximum impact on the people around her. It sounded different and foreign to her ears. To cover her surprise, she moved to mop up the mess with the napkins on the table. When Rosa gathered herself together again, she went inside to get more tea. She came out with a paper cup and a bag.

"I put a cinnamon roll in there. I made too many yesterday, and I don't like to sell anything more than a day old."

Annabelle hadn't ever experienced such free giving, and she didn't know what to do with it, so she muttered another thank you and headed down the street toward the river. It occurred to her as she left that she hadn't paid for breakfast in years, and here she paid twice at Rosa's, and still Rosa gave her extra on top. The thought was distinctly uncomfortable, so when she passed the next street stand, she slid a beaded necklace off the side into her pocket while the owner wasn't looking. She would never wear it, but taking it made her feel more like herself.

Partway to the river, you notice someone sliding in next to you and walking in step. You look up, and Pedro is there, looking surly. You remember the fight of the night before. He would need something from you in order to calm the air between you. With a sigh of regret, you hand over the paper bag with the cinnamon roll. With Rosa's delectable baking, you're certain it's the best cinnamon roll ever made, but sacrifices must be made to keep the status quo. Pedro opens the bag and eyes it greedily.

"Do you have anything else for me?" He asked her.

"No. Why, what are you talking about?" She was irritated about the cinnamon roll and didn't feel like playing his games.

"A schedule. I'm asking if you have a schedule." There was an edge to his voice she didn't like.

"No," she answered curtly, then continued with a glint of satisfaction in her voice, "But I have a plan."

CHAPTER 6

Chapter 6—Day 5

The plan is simple enough. Caretaker, above all else, loves to take care of people. All you need to do is find a wheelchair and fake a leg injury. An ankle brace at the corner store should do the trick. Then play it up big like it's keeping you from working the docks. Tell Caretaker you've been spending time in the garden to be close to the Keeper, and you saw hurt people going in and coming out healed, but you need help getting in with the wheelchair.

$\mathcal{A}$nnabelle stood outside the corner store, hair dyed back to her original deep brown, brushed smooth, and a touch of makeup on her face. She put on the good suit she reserved for times like this—when she needed to make a score fast. Clothes were everything when it came to conning people. Of course, for Caretaker to believe she wanted to be working the docks, she would need to make a quick change to her coveralls. She breathed deeply to slow her heart rate and walked into the store for all the world as if she were a paying customer. She browsed for a while, checking out different makeup before she headed to the medical section. She looked through the ankle braces. All the boxes were too bulky to hide in her suit, so she pulled it out, making it look like she was checking sizes. When the cashier was busy with another customer, she made a big show of putting something in the box and closing it, but instead, she slid the brace inside her suit coat. As she walked out, she waved cheerfully, shrugged, and said, "Wrong size." The cashier simply waved back.

Now, all she needed was a wheelchair. She knew of no better place to find one than at the hospital, which was close to the Keeper's court and not too far from Caretaker's house. Wheelchairs could be tricky because the people who had them were generally using them. But it was still her best shot. Stealing one from a store wasn't really an option on such short notice and without help. *I should've sent Pedro for the wheelchair. He could do something for this plan for once.* It's too late for that. She neared the hospital, glad she was still in her navy suit. The ER was pretty busy today, which suited her purposes just fine. She walked in and found a blustering, older woman behind the counter. She was struggling with the computer system. Annabelle leaned over the young man with a bleeding hand to interrupt. Flustered people in a hurry were the easiest to con.

"Excuse me, I'm in need of some assistance immediately please, it's my grandmother." Annabelle assumed the look of a dutiful and worried granddaughter.

"I'll get someone to you in just a moment, dearie! They're all helping other patients right now." The blustery woman grimaced compassionately to Annabelle.

"Oh, no! Oh no, it really is a pretty big rush. She's not breathing so well. Can I just take one of those wheelchairs out to her and bring her in myself?"

The woman sighed with relief, "Oh yes! That's a wonderful idea, thank you! It's been a madhouse in here all day!"

Annabelle rushed over to an empty wheelchair at the entrance and pushed it out, looking like she was going to do exactly what she said.

But when she reached the further end of the parking lot, she just kept going. Let them wonder what happened to the poor grandmother who couldn't breathe. She turned a corner and breathed a sigh of relief. The ankle brace and wheelchair— done! Really, the easy parts were done. It was always easier to pull something on someone who wasn't suspicious of her already. Caretaker wouldn't be easy to fool! At that thought, she almost turned back. She didn't want to see Caretaker again. Caretaker would want to talk about what happened and why she left. About why she never let anyone know where she was. If only Caretaker would have read her Future Book when she threw it at her. Then she would know why already, at least as much as Annabelle did herself. She did everything she did because the book said so. It was the next move to make. And she didn't mind the freedom that came with it either—no more answering for her lying or stealing. No one cared.

As you push the wheelchair up a hill on the way to Caretaker's house, sweat breaks out on your upper lip. Part of it was the warm day, but you know, deep inside, the other part is because you're nervous about how Caretaker will respond to you. Five chapters in the Future Book have passed since you saw her last, well, until last night. The thing about Caretaker is that she had other people in her care before you. You know the stories of how those people ran off and came back. Caretaker was always, always glad to see them. Most of them broke her heart again, some more than once. You cringe just a little at the thought that you'll be one of the repeat offenders.

Annabelle shook her head against the feeling of guilt. She had to get across that bridge *soon* if she was going to live to see another chapter. This was the quickest way she could think of to make that happen.

She needed to get inside that building to find out when the truck was leaving and what route it took.

There was a gas station around the corner from Caretaker's house. Annabelle left the wheelchair in the trees behind it and ducked inside to change. She took off the suit coat and dress shirt and put her coveralls over her tank top and pants. On the way out, she swiped a pathetic bunch of flowers near the door. Always bring a gift when you need something. Caretaker loved gifts, it should soften her up. She moved the wheelchair to the parking lot and sat down in it to remove her left shoe and lace up the ankle brace. She groaned at the thought of using her arms to get that wheelchair up the hill by Caretaker's house, but she didn't have a choice. She had to play the part, and if Caretaker was watching out any windows, she would know. Annabelle set about heaving herself up the steep hill. By the time the road evened out, she was sweating profusely. She pulled up in front of the Caretaker's house, but it looked different. Caretaker was great with people but couldn't keep flowers alive. The house had flowers *everywhere*. She could see them all across the front of the house. Annabelle knew before she knocked on the door that Caretaker wasn't going to be there anymore. But she knocked anyway, just in case. A shorter, sweet-looking woman answered the door.

"I'm so sorry; I was looking for my Caretaker, I thought she lived here!"

"No, you must be mistaken. I've lived here for the past year and a half."

Annabelle didn't want to admit she didn't know where her Caretaker was, but she couldn't see any way around it if she was going to get any information from the lady standing before her. She scrambled for a plausible story.

"What could have happened to her? When I left for the mainland, she was right here! I've been out doing the Keeper's business on the mainland. We've shared a couple of letters, but it was hard to stay in contact. Do you know where she went? Did she leave any message for me?" Annabelle cringed. It was weak, at best.

The lady stared at her through her fumbling story as if she had no idea what she was talking about. Then she slowly turned, calling out a "Wait here" over her retreating back. Annabelle couldn't even begin to hope Caretaker had left her a message. The lady was back soon with a folded piece of paper.

"Are you Desiree?"

"Yes! Yes, I am! Oh, thank goodness, I've been missing her so, so much. I couldn't stand the thought of not finding her!" Annabelle truly had no idea who Desiree could be. It must be someone else that Caretaker had taken care of through the years. Well, if she hadn't come back by now, she probably never would. Annabelle held out her hand for the paper, and the lady handed it to her.

"Well, I'm glad to have that delivered. She was so anxious to have that one taken care of. I know it killed her to move away where you couldn't find her, Desiree."

Annabelle wondered for a moment if Caretaker had even thought about her when she moved to a new place with no forwarding address. But why would she even bother? *I guess I made it pretty clear I wouldn't be back. Still, it's like I didn't mean anything to her at all.*

"Thank you. I'll get out of your hair now, Ma'am." She didn't know if the lady ever saw Caretaker, so she wheeled herself until she was back to the trees behind the gas station. Then she pulled out the paper and opened it.

My dearest Desiree, it read, *The Keeper said you would need me, and I should leave you a way to find me. He didn't say how long you would be, and that's ok. You can find me near the Keeper's Garden, to the east. You'll know it when you see it! And you know I'm always here for you. ~Caretaker*

Annabelle tossed the paper into the woods and, as an afterthought, also tossed the scraggly flowers after it. She started thinking through the new complications of her plan. She couldn't wander the streets near the garden in a wheelchair. Who knows how long it would take to find the Caretaker's new place! But she couldn't walk the streets either since she was sure to be seen. She would need to wait it out in the garden, keeping an eye on the gate. Caretaker had gone once, she was sure to go again. But that meant keeping a watch through the night. She'd need sleep first and couldn't go to her box during the day.

She quickly decided to head back to the river and nap in her chair. She could head over to the garden when she woke up. Looking at the wheelchair, Annabelle groaned. What to do with this clunky thing? She couldn't very well take it all over town with her. She spotted a thick spot in the trees and tucked the wheelchair back where it was mostly hidden from the road. That would have to do for now! Annabelle brushed the stray leaves off her coveralls and headed back to the river, swiping a bottle on her way there.

You wake up as the sun goes down. Before you went to sleep, you put your chair in the shade, but the path of the sun had traveled to your face. You felt the familiar burn and knew your cheeks were bright pink from sunburn. You tell yourself if Caretaker doesn't come tonight that, you'll have to be more careful tomorrow. Hunger rips through your belly, the fruit you had for breakfast a faint memory now. Knowing you need something to sustain you through the night, you decide on a small market where you know you can find trail mix and jerky to munch on. You make quick work of lifting the snacks and an iced tea and make your way to the Keeper's garden, still in your coveralls. When you get to the garden, you don't head for your usual low wall and tree. You can't be seen this time, so you find a patch of grass on the edge of the garden. It's in the trees and behind some bushes and you make your nest. Something about it feels familiar.

Annabelle looked around her overgrown hiding place and wondered why this would feel familiar. She was a city girl to the max and hadn't spent much time at all in any sort of nature. In her younger years, she had been terrified of bees, and there were enough around to keep her inside semi-permanently. She looked behind her at a barely visible path in the dirt, and slowly, the dream came back to her. The eyes of her protector, streaming with tears, flooded her vision. Looking back toward the garden, she realized she was behind the cow statue. *Stop it!* She screamed inside her mind. She had a job to do, and nothing was going to distract her. Least of all, a crazy dream. She turned her mind to making a break in the leaves wide enough to see the gate through without being too wide and giving her away.

Clouds roll in and cover what's left of the sunset. They completely obliterate the moon. You're still able to see the few people moving about, but just as forms and shadows. Luckily, you know the Caretaker's silhouette by heart. A form moves through the garden, hesitating by the gate but eventually moving on without entering. Even with today's nap, you're fighting the drooping of your eyelids. Pulling out the trail mix, you begin to munch, thinking it's going to be a long, long night.

Thinking through the plan, you wonder if it's even worth it to try to find Caretaker. Maybe a stranger would be better? But then again, there was such high security at that gate. Surely, no one would bring a stranger with them through it. The old woman and the young man had clearly been close to each other. No, you need Caretaker to bring you through. You just hope you find her before the load of books goes across to the other island. Once that happens, you're out of options. There's no plan beyond that.

I could come up with one, though. Why should I stick to one long-shot plan to change my fate? There must be another way. She thought and thought, interrupted only now and then by another shadow making its way to the garden gate. None of them were the familiar form of Caretaker, and Annabelle grew frustrated with both the waiting and the fruitless brainstorming. There really was no Plan B. And why would there be? The book said there wasn't!

A rustle on the overgrown path behind her made Annabelle's heart leap. She froze as the rustle grew closer and then recognized the familiar presence of the Messenger. Behind her was someone tall and gangly. Annabelle thought desperately about how to explain hiding in the back of the garden but came up blank. She needn't have worried, though. The messenger dropped an envelope in her lap and moved on past. The young man following the messenger, however, dropped down to sit next to her.

CHAPTER 7

Chapter 6—Day 6

Off in the distance, you hear the bells announce the midnight hour. Still, the young man didn't speak. You recognize him now as the man from Rosa's Cafe, the one with a Lion seal on his uniform pocket. What had the Watcher called him? Oh yes, the Comforter. His presence was more unsettling than comforting at the moment. You shiver and pull your legs up to your chest. Impatience and frustration get the better of you.

"This is a public space, you know. And as far as I've heard, it never closes. I have every right to be here," Annabelle snapped into the silence.

The young man roared with laughter, surprising her. "Why yes! Everyone is welcome in the garden of the Keeper."

"Okay, then... What are you doing here?"

"Am I not welcome in the Keeper's garden? I thought I was part of everyone." He threw her a cheeky grin. Clearly, he was enjoying himself.

"No, why are you here? Why have you plopped yourself down in my little area here?!?" Annabelle gestured to the small circle she had created in the leaves.

"I gotta tell you, I really don't know. Usually, the messenger brings me to people who are all weepy and crying—ya know, ones who are in pain. But you seem to be just fine, all bristly and hard. Why do you think the messenger brought me here?" He grinned at her, completely at ease.

Annabelle wasn't. "How would I know?" She snapped.

"Well," the Comforter yawned, "if you read your message, you might know. Personally, I was in a nice deep sleep, and I'd rather do this in the morning over coffee. Want to meet me at Rosa's for breakfast?"

"What!? Why would I meet you for breakfast?" Annabelle looked back to the envelope in her lap. She was tired of the messenger's envelopes.

"I'm going to take that as a no on breakfast. Guess I'll need to stay up. You don't happen to have some snacks to help me stay awake? I'm starving!" He tipped his head sideways and smiled at her hopefully, pointing to the bag of trail mix. Without thinking, Annabelle tipped the bag toward him so he could reach inside. "Thanks! You're so prickly tonight I wasn't sure you'd give me any!"

Rude. "You're the one in my space! I've got every right to… to… to prickle!" Annabelle sputtered the last words out. The Comforter laughed again, a sort of hiccup-like laugh that made him seem younger. Annabelle was tempted to laugh with him but restrained herself. Suddenly realizing the talking and laughter were probably giving her hiding spot away, she straightened and stared silently at the gate again. The Comforter settled down and munched quietly on Annabelle's trail mix. For a while, the only noise in the garden was the crunch of his chewing.

He leaned over with a conspiratorial whisper, "What are we waiting for?"

"For you to leave," she snapped back at him.

Again, he laughed. "I can't! The Messenger brought me here; it must be for a reason. Why don't you open the message and figure it out so we both know, and then I can do it and go?"

Annabelle picked up the envelope from the Messenger between two fingers and raised an eyebrow at it. The messages she got were never helpful for the things she was working on. She did want the Comforter to go away, but he would get tired of sitting there eventually anyway. She half-tossed it over to the Comforter and said, "Well, if you're so anxious to know what the Messenger had to say tonight, you read it!"

The Comforter picked up the card from where it fell in the grass between them and tried to hand it back to her. "That's not how they work, and you know it."

Annabelle looked down at the envelope he was now poking into her arm and turned her attention back to the gate once again. She couldn't miss Caretaker tonight. Every day brought her death closer. She felt the time rushing away from her and, with it, any chance to change her fate.

"Do you want to talk about it?" The Comforter asked casually from a mouth full of trail mix.

"Talk about what?"

"Whatever it is that has your forehead all crinkly and your mouth all puckered! Want to talk about it? I'm a great listener." He gave her a cheeky grin.

"No."

"Are you sure? It took me a long time to become a good listener. I really rather enjoy the talking side of things. I could talk all night! Pick a topic; I'll have an opinion. And then we can debate whose opinion is better and why mine is right. But I've been spending a lot of time with the Messenger, and she's been showing me when to talk and when to listen. You should've seen the first time she tried to get me to listen to someone. I couldn't stop jumping in any time they took a breath. Boy, that was a day. I think we spent all day with that guy before he finally explained what his trouble was. He just couldn't get a whole line out without taking a breath, and of course, I jumped in and tried to finish his sentences, but Whoa! Was I wrong about what was bothering him? I kept thinking it was something to do with his younger brother when really it was about his grandmother's poodle. Every time I tried to ask him about his younger brother, he got really confused, and then I got even more confused, and somehow, we ended up talking about our favorite places to go out to eat. He didn't get to the point until like 10 that night, and then it all ended up being about that silly poodle. Which I guess wasn't silly to him because it wasn't silly to his grandmother, and she was getting quite old and very lonely, except for the dog. But the dog was getting old and sick. It was a whole thing. But anyway, do you want to talk about it? I'm all ears."

"You're a good listener, eh?" Annabelle rolled her eyes.

"Yes! I've worked super hard on that. So. You're feeling all crinkly and pucker-y. Want to tell me what that's all about?"

"Uh, no."

"So, what you're telling me is that I have to sit here all night, and you're not going to read the envelope and tell me why. And you're not going to share what's going on. And you won't meet me at Rosa's in the morning instead so I can sleep. So I'm stuck here with you." He looked thoughtful for a moment, then he perked up and said, "Ok! What do you want me to talk about then?"

"What?!?"

"'What' is an interesting word, but I'm not sure I can talk about it all night. We could talk about our favorite places to eat? Personally, Rosa's is my absolute favorite! It's about more than the food there. It's Rosa herself. There's something special about her. She makes you feel like you're the only person in the world. It's like she cares way more than most people. Don't you think? And the way she's brightening up that street with her flowers and how it's decorated. It's just homey and happy at the same time. What? What is it?" Annabelle had been shushing him.

"Listen, you need to be quiet if you're going to stay. I'm trying to... um..."

"You're trying to what? Meditate? Sleep? You're sitting up; it's kind of a hard position to sleep in!"

"PLEASE stop talking!"

"Ok, I'll stop. Your turn. Tell me anything."

"Ok, I will. Are you ready to listen?"

The Comforter made a motion like he was zipping his lips shut and nodded.

"Here it is: SHUT UP!"

Motion in the garden near the gate drew Annabelle's attention. The shape *could* have been Caretaker. She squinted, trying to see more clearly.

"If I shut up, though, neither one of us will be talking, and I probably *will* fall asleep themmmphfhf." His words were cut off as Annabelle covered his mouth with her hand. She drew the other across her throat in an effort to warn him off of speaking further. But as soon as she lifted her hand, he began again, "Like I was saying, then I'll fall asleep. I can't very well go back to the Messenger and report *that* to her!"

He wasn't a quiet speaker and Caretaker turned and looked toward the bushes where they hid. Then she shrugged and opened the gate, and headed inside.

"Aaaauuuugghh! You are infuriating! Why are you here!!!" Annabelle released all her frustration into pounding on his shoulder.

The Comforter laughed as he deftly deflected her blows. "I believe I've already told you; the answer is in the note from the Messenger. If you read it, then we'll both know."

"No! I've had enough of the Messenger's notes. I don't want to know. I'm done reading them. And you just need to leave!" Annabelle started moving her things back into her backpack in preparation for Caretaker's return. She would need to move fast and quietly to find out where Caretaker lived now.

The Comforter stared at her sadly for a moment, then stood without a word. From her crouched position, he looked as tall as the statues. He turned toward the gate and ambled over, leaving

Annabelle. As he reached the gate, Caretaker emerged. She had spent much less time in there tonight.

You watch as the Comforter greets Caretaker. She looks old tonight. The Comforter holds out his arm to her, and she takes it with a small smile. Together, they leave the garden by the front entrance. You're torn; the Comforter knows where you are. He could reveal you at any moment. But you've got to get the location of Caretaker's house if you're going to pull off the next part of the plan. You take three steps toward the front of the garden, then change your mind and leave through the back alley. No sense in giving yourself away. There will be another night. You leave the note from the Messenger lying in the grass, unopened.

You wake up in your box just hours later. It still isn't enough sleep, especially since you need to pull another all-nighter in the garden. It can't be helped, though; you have to vacate the area. You change into a light dress and grab some more change. Rosa's is on the way to the garden, and that's where you'll need to be. You still have a chance of overhearing someone discussing the truck schedule. Perking up at the thought of Rosa's pastries, you lift your backpack and head in that direction.

Rosa's was busy that morning, but Annabelle still found a seat outside. She was surrounded by young moms with small kids. The air was filled with the boisterous giggles of children and the chatter of moms eager for adult conversation. Annabelle watched enviously. If only she had been given a different role to play, she could have been one of the moms with a sweet child of her own or a caretaker watching over someone else's while they grew. Instead of the usual lift of her spirits, this trip dragged her down into the mire of hopelessness and rage.

Just then, Rosa interrupted the downward spiral with a cheerful smile, "Welcome back! I'll get your tea in just a moment. And can I tempt you with another cinnamon roll?"

"Yes, that would be great."

"Ok! Let me grab the dishes from the second table, and I'll get right on that!" Rosa's smile was genuine, and Annabelle couldn't help but respond to it.

Rosa was back in no time with piping hot tea and a warm cinnamon roll with melted icing dripping off the sides. "Here you go, sweetheart! These cinnamon rolls are so much better, fresh and warm. I just know you're gonna love it!"

"Thank you, Rosa." The end of the name rose like a question.

"Yes, I'm Rosa! And what's your name?"

"I'm Annabelle."

"You know, Annabelle, I could really use some extra help around here. This place has just gotten busier and busier, especially with the morning rush. If you'd ever be interested in a job, let me know. Now you enjoy that cinnamon roll before it gets cold!" With a wave and another smile, Rosa moved on to another table, leaving Annabelle to wonder if she actually heard her right. Nobody had ever offered her so much so freely. She ate her cinnamon roll slowly, relishing every moment of deliciousness. She left enough change on the table to pay for the tea and roll and moved on her way to the garden. Thinking about the cinnamon roll made her think about the other one she had sacrificed to Pedro, and thinking about Pedro made her realize she hadn't seen him. With a groan, she turned toward the river instead. She was sure he would be angry if she hadn't checked in.

You're right; he is angry. When you walk up, you can

see the look on his face and feel the tension. He's clenching and unclenching one fist, and the other is balled inside a pocket. You realize you don't have a pacifier this time, and you haven't made enough progress on the plan. You start to get a little panicky.

"Where have you been!" Pedro roared at her, striding toward her angrily.

"Cool it, Pedro. You don't own me." Annabelle cringed. That was definitely the wrong thing to say if she wanted him to calm down. She didn't know why she said it, but then she remembered it was what had been in the Future Book. Why did she always do the *worst* things?!?

"Listen to me, chica; you do not tell me to 'cool it.' I set up the buyers, so I make the calls. And my buyers are getting nervous. I don't have anything to tell them, and they are ready to split. So I need an update, *ahora, Chiquita.*"

What did the book say she did next? Annabelle couldn't remember. The writing was getting fuzzy again, but that could be because she was feeling stressed. Her heart rate was rising, and her breathing was shallow. Trying to maintain, she began taking deep breaths, but the tunnel vision was starting to creep in.

"Listen, I don't have an update. I do have a plan, but it got messed up because Caretaker *moved* and didn't leave a forwarding address. But I know where she goes every night, so I can find out where she lives and take the plan forward from there." She spat it all out in one breath and then heaved the next breath in. Anxiety wrapped itself around her heart and left her hands shaking. Pedro grabbed her wrist and squeezed it.

"You need to calm down, now." The threat in his voice was palpable, but in case she didn't get the picture, he also pulled out his knife and clicked it open. Annabelle gulped in the air and dug her fingernails into her palm, trying desperately to ground herself. But the sight of the knife brought her last day to mind once again, and she began to cry.

"Please, I'll have something for you tomorrow morning. I'll have the date of the shipment. I promise." She tried to pull her wrist away, but he was too strong.

"You have 24 hours to get me what I need to know. I'm tired of carrying you. If you don't get me what I want, I'm through."

His words break through the anxiety fog and through the tears. You wish with everything you have that he was telling the truth. You wish he would just leave and never come back. You wish you could. Instead, you promise him again you'll have everything he needs and beg him to be patient and to let you go.

Annabelle said, "No," in a loud voice. The sound surprised and sobered her. *How did I do that? That's not what the book says! Oh, Keeper, I can't say that! He's going to kill me now instead of later!* The panic gave her the strength to wrench her wrist out of his grasp. She backtracked. "N-n-no problem. You'll have exactly what you need by this time tomorrow. I just need you to be patient until then. Please." Her words seemed to mollify him. He smiled at her, happy in the knowledge that he still held the power.

"Alright, princess," he smirked, "I think we understand each other." He reached out and pulled her close, intoxicated by her groveling. He rubbed his fingers up and down the outside of her arm and breathed deeply with his face buried in her hair. Ignoring her stiff muscles, he led her under the bridge.

You follow his lead and do everything he asks of you. Your mind is elsewhere, however, as you sort through your twenty-four-hour ultimatum from Pedro.

Twenty-four hours isn't enough to guarantee you would have the information. You need to get him to extend the time frame. But how? You'll have to give him something else he wants.

Money. But how much money would she need to give him? Annabelle quickly calculated what was left in her jar and knew it wasn't enough. She panned through the places with easy access and ample cash and couldn't find one she could steal from in the next twenty-four hours.

You adjust your clothing and begin to barter for more time. He will take five hundred and no less. You scream inwardly. You knew it would be an astronomical number but you have to have the extra time. There was no way around it. You agree, either five hundred or the truck schedule tomorrow mid-morning. The cash would buy you one more day. The deal helps you breathe easier, but you will still need a quick score. An awful idea appears in your mind. One that you hate but can't deny. You know of one place where you could get quick access to enough cash. Rosa's cheerful smile slides into your mind, and you groan.

Annabelle argued with herself the entire walk back to Rosa's. There had to be another source of money, but she couldn't think of one that was guaranteed. She hated losing Rosa's as a morning stop, but she could easily go back to stealing fruit once the score was made. She would need to get hired *today* to make it work. She was walking so fast she didn't notice the Messenger in front of her until she ran right into her. The Messenger was holding out an envelope; the look on her face hadn't changed, but it felt like she was weary. Annabelle took the note and kept walking. Thinking maybe the Messenger was going to give her a different mark, she ripped open the envelope. The card was blank, so she flipped it over. The back was just as empty. Confused, Annabelle turned to find the Messenger had already gone from view.

Well. That's about as helpful as the rest of your messages. Whatever. She dropped the envelope and card on the side of the road and kept going. She let the anger take over. She honed it until it was useful to her. And when she got to Rosa's, she greeted her with a wide-eyed smile.

CHAPTER 8

Chapter 6—Day 7, midnight

Rosa hired you on sight. You volunteered to start right away and work the morning shift the next day. The rest of the day was filled with learning the kitchen and the dining room. You learned how to make the delectable crois-sants. She gave you the code to the cash register. You smiled through it all, even clean-up after the cafe closed. Rosa was so grateful for the help and eagerly said, "See you in the morning!" You didn't let doubt drag you down for a single moment. When work was done, you crashed into your chair by the bridge. You wake up and make your way once again to the hidden place in the garden.

If all goes well tonight, I won't even need to go to Rosa's tomorrow. Annabelle was tired from waiting on tables and cleaning all day, but it was a much nicer place to work than the docks. Everyone was smiling and happy, and Rosa was a firm but gentle manager. She had high standards, but she was encouraging and pleasant. *Maybe I will go back anyway.* Her thoughts were interrupted by a rustle in the leaves next to her. Annabelle rolled her eyes.

"What are you doing here?" She asked the Keeper's agent, The Comforter.

"Really? We're going to play that game again?" He felt around on the ground until his hand landed on the damp envelope, which he picked up and handed to her again.

"Listen. I'm not in the mood for this. I have something important going on, and I really need to concentrate. I can't have any distractions!! You need to go." Annabelle grabbed the envelope and tossed it backward over her shoulder.

"Oh, no, of course, I don't want to get in your way. Shall we meet at Rosa's tomorrow morning instead?"

"What? No!" Panic filled Annabelle's thoughts. If he were there in the morning, she wouldn't be able to steal the money she needed. "No, absolutely not. But I don't want to see you now either! Just leave me alone!"

"Aw, I'm sorry, I can't do that. The Messenger sent me here. I think the Watcher is coming later, too. Oh wait, is that him? Hey, Adler! Over here!" He stood up and waved to the other agent who had just entered the garden.

"Liev! Hello, sir! I couldn't see you for a minute." The two men embraced, thumping each other on the back. Annabelle could tell they were brothers despite the difference in their appearance. Just then, the Watcher noticed her sitting there. "Oh, hi, Annabelle! You sure spend a lot of time in the garden." His eyes sparkled, and his smile was wide and genuine.

Annabelle groaned dramatically and flopped back in the soft grass. A thought occurred to her then, "Wait," she said from her position on the ground, "You guys have names? I thought you were just called 'Watcher' and 'Comforter.'"

The agents sat down, one on either side of Annabelle, and Adler spoke up, "Well, we weren't always the Keeper's agents. I mean, we were chosen pretty young, but we had names first. Most people don't know them, though, I guess. Allow me to re-introduce myself! My name is Adler. Adler, the eagle-eye Watcher. And this here is Liev, the lion-heart Comforter."

"Hi," Annabelle waved limply, still lying on the ground.

Liev looked over to Adler, "So, what are you up to tonight? The Messenger told me you'd be coming, but she didn't say why."

Adler shrugged. "Honestly? I don't know yet. Usually, I do, but this time, all she said was to come here and stay until the job was clear. She's usually a little more specific in her instructions. What about you? Maybe it's the job you're doing?"

Liev laughed, "Well, I don't know either. The Messenger gave instructions to Annabelle here," he fumbled around in the grass and found the envelope yet again, "but she won't open it! So I'm as in the dark as you are."

Adler grabbed the envelope and examined it. "Umm, Annabelle? The Writer doesn't send instructions lightly. He's pretty serious about it. And you wouldn't know it, but it breaks the Messenger's heart every time someone ignores her notes."

Annabelle groaned again and sat up, "Her notes never make any sense! And the last one she gave me didn't have anything on it at all! It was empty!"

Both men furrowed their brows and stared at her. Liev's jaw hung open. He began to stutter, "You... you... you mean..."

The Watcher spoke up, "What my brother is trying to say is, you mean there was nothing at all written there? Not even the faintest of letters?"

"Nothing," Annabelle replied, with a little less ferocity. The way the brothers were looking at her made her wonder if she had done something terribly wrong.

"Adler! She... she... she..." The Comforter was dumbstruck and looked as if all the air had been let out of him.

"Liev, pull yourself together, man. You've seen this before. It's not hopeless, just..." Adler lifted his hands, palms up. For a moment, Annabelle was distracted by the red mark on his right hand. "Well, as you can see, Miss Annabelle, you've left Comforter chatterbox here speechless. And as you can imagine, that's not an easy feat!"

Annabelle snorted despite herself. "You can say that again!"

"So, we've got ourselves a little problem here. You really need to see what the Writer sent you, but my guess is that you've been ignoring the messages for a while now. Is that fair?" Adler's usually bright eyes were stormy.

As Annabelle listened, she grew more and more impatient with their presence. Yes, she had been ignoring the messages, but they didn't make any sense anyway. And she had a job to do. One that didn't leave room for them to be there. "Guys, listen. I don't have time for this. I've got things to do, and it's actually really important that I get them done. So I really need you to leave, Liev, and take the Watcher with you!!"

Now it was Liev's turn to snort. "Leave, leave? You want me to leave twice?" He and Adler laughed together while Annabelle fumed.

"YES. Leave twice. Leave three times. Just GO!" she yelled. It was getting close to the time that Caretaker showed up twice before and she needed them to go.

"Hey, Annabelle, I feel like you missed the part where we're here under orders," Adler started, but Liev jumped in, "Yes! And there's no way you're getting rid of us! So, you might as well tell us what this important mission of yours is. Maybe we can help?"

"Or," Adler jumped back in, "we could figure out why her notes are blank and help her get back in touch with the Messenger."

"Believe me," Liev replied, "you're barking up the wrong tree with that one. She wants nothing to do with the Messenger or the Keeper. It's pretty obvious when they can't even see the words anymore. She won't even open the envelope! There's no way she's going to let us dig into that!!"

Annabelle, who had been watching them both carefully, noticed a look of surprise on Adler's face and wondered why.

"Liev, you know you can't give up on her."

"I know. And I won't. I just don't see it getting through to her right now. She's going to have to be a lot more desperate before she's ready to listen."

Annabelle listened to the exchange with growing fury. "Stop it! Stop talking about me like I'm not even here! And how would you know what I'm ready for and what I'm not? I'll do what I want to do. You don't think I'll open that envelope or listen, well, I'll show you." She snatched the envelope up and ripped down the side, sliding out the card inside.

Adler and Liev watched silently as she flipped the card over.

"Nothing. Again." Annabelle felt the agent's despair in that moment. She didn't even want a message from the Writer. Relief washed over her. Despite her bravado, she had been a bit worried about what the message would say this time. What if it was telling her to stop what she was trying to do? Then, the Watcher and Comforter would know she wasn't on the right side of the law. What would they do then? They're agents of the Keeper. She would be in trouble for sure.

Adler held out his hand, "Can I see it?"

"Why not? There's nothing there." Annabelle handed him the card.

Adler examined it closely. There wasn't a lot of light—the moon had been hidden in the clouds for a while now—but Adler had excellent vision. "No, there's actually something here, but I can't quite make it out."

Liev perked up. "You mean it's not all the way gone?"

Adler smiled at him, "No, it's faint, but it's here. All we have to do is figure out why it's so faint and then we can help her get back to reading her messages again."

"I don't WANT to read them." Annabelle snatched the card back and stuffed it inside her backpack.

Adler grimaced, then stood and said, "Well, I've got my job cut out for me, don't I? It's been a pleasure, folks, but it's time for me to go."

"Good." Annabelle snapped.

"Oh, I see," said Liev. "Well, good luck to ya! Let me know if I can help, and definitely let me know when you've accomplished your mission. Looks like I've got some more long nights ahead of me while you do that." He stood up and shook Adler's hand.

"While you're taking your leave, you wouldn't want to take your Liev, too?" Annabelle cackled at her own joke.

"Hey, she's kinda funny. At least your night won't be boring." Adler waved and headed out of the garden.

"You sure you don't want to go with him? Bet he's headed home to a nice soft bed somewhere!" Annabelle pleaded with the Comforter.

"Ugh. Yes, yes, I do, actually." The Comforter replied grumpily.

"Ya know, since we haven't been able to read the Messenger's note, maybe you should just wait for Adler to do his thing. We can pick this up another time, right? No need to stay when you don't know what it is you're doing here anyway. And I'm sure it won't take Adler long to fix it, right? There's no sense in you missing all that sleep."

"Hmm, that almost makes sense. But I'll stay. I'm sure the Messenger has a reason for me to be here."

Annabelle drooped. Her hopes of finding Caretaker's house tonight dwindled. She realized then she would have to get the money from Rosa's in the morning even if she found where Caretaker lived that night. She wouldn't have time to get Caretaker to get her inside before her twenty-four-hour deadline was up. Not that it would be hard to take it from Rosa's. Rosa was way too trusting. It would be simple to swipe what she needed from the register while Rosa was outside serving someone. And from there she would just need to tell her she wasn't feeling well or something. Still, that cash would only buy her another day. She needed to follow Caretaker *tonight*.

Having settled her mind, she turned her attention to the gate. Someone was coming out of it, and she peered through the bushes to see who it was. To her surprise, it was a child, no more than five or six years old. *How did they get in?* Annabelle traced the white mark on her hand, wondering again why it didn't work for her.

Annabelle watched and waited. She was so focused on her mission that she forgot all about the Comforter sitting next to her. A couple hours passed, and several people came and went, but none of them were Caretaker. After a while, she stood to stretch and looked over at

Liev. He was curled up on his side, sound asleep. She laughed quietly, finished stretching, and sat back down. *Now,* she could do what she needed to do. Just then, Caretaker walked into the garden and entered through the gate.

Annabelle stealthily rose, picked up her backpack, and double-checked to see that the Comforter was still asleep. She unwrapped the sweatshirt from around her waist and carefully covered his shoulders with it, then stood with a tree between her and the gate, barely looking out to be able to see it. For this to work, she absolutely could not be seen.

The Caretaker took her time in the room behind the gate that night. Annabelle yawned as she waited. It had been a long day, and she was getting tired. She envied the Comforter for his cozy place on the grass and his peaceful sleep. Mid-yawn, she heard the clank of the gate. Caretaker moved quickly, looking younger today. The moon peaked out and highlighted her sun-bleached hair. Annabelle moved to follow her, sticking to the shadows and remaining about a block behind. She followed her for about five blocks before she turned into a small side street. Annabelle waited at the corner for a moment before she turned. The street was empty. Annabelle knew that meant she lived somewhere on this block. To be safe, she went back to the main road and loitered there for a while before heading back to the street. The note had said Desiree would know the house when she saw it, so Annabelle was assuming she would, too.

You walk slowly down the street, studying each house with care, but nothing strikes you as belonging to Care-taker. You see houses with plants, houses with statues, and ones with swing sets in the backyard. You walk up and down the street twice before you see it: the small house at the end of the street. The side door has a half-window on the top, and the inside light is on. Through the window you see the top part of a mural—it looks like a

75

desert scene. Caretaker painted everything and loved to fill her house with murals. It has to be her place. Still, you wonder if that's enough for Desiree to identify the house. Why would Caretaker say it's so obvious?

Annabelle slid over by the tree in the front yard, studying the front of the house carefully. Hanging from the ceiling of the small front porch was a wind chime of small carved wooden objects. Annabelle didn't recognize it, but it could have been given to Caretaker by Desiree for all she knew. It was the only other defining feature of the house, so that had to be it. Either way, she was certain she had found it. She could go get some sleep now. She moved fast and settled into her box. She didn't love the thought of waking up in a couple of hours to get to Rosa's, but it couldn't be helped. After she stole the money, she could get it to Pedro and find a place to nap for a while.

The morning comes all too soon and you lay in bed for as long as you dare. At the last minute, you get up and put on a clean dress. It feels good to stretch your legs as you make the walk to Rosa's. It doesn't take long to get there, and Rosa is delighted to see you.

"Annabelle! I'm so glad you're here. Can you start setting up the front seating area? I'm just pulling the early baking out of the oven. I'm so, so happy to have help now! It's been getting busier and busier, and I just couldn't keep up by myself." Rosa had flour on her forehead and in her hair. She opened the oversized oven and started taking out the baked goods. She burned her forearm on the oven shelf but hardly reacted at all.

Annabelle lurched forward, "Rosa, your arm is burned, you should run that under some cold water!"

Rosa set down the tray and lifted one shoulder with a nonchalant air. "Oh, I do that all the time." And she held her arms out as proof.

Several burn scars striped her forearm. She moved to the sink and ran the cold water over the newest one. When she was finished, she turned back to the tray of croissants she had just pulled out. She picked one up and handed it to Annabelle. "Have you had breakfast yet?"

"No, I slept late! Thank you." Annabelle devoured the croissant, then said, "Well, I guess I'll get to setting up the front."

Rosa keeps you busy setting up. When the shop opens, you start out front taking orders and bussing tables. You keep looking for a chance to get to the register, but Rosa stays there most of the morning. Eventually, you come up with a plan to get her away from the register for long enough to grab the cash. A lull in customers gives you the chance you need, and you head inside.

"Rosa, the morning rush has slowed down. Would you like to take a break? I can handle things here." Annabelle smiled at her encouragingly. "When's the last time you had a break?"

Rosa laughed, "I can't recall ever having one! I think I'll take you up on that. I'll just be upstairs for a few. You sure you've got things here?"

"Oh yes, no problem at all! Go take that break."

Rosa went to the back of the store and up the stairs. Annabelle wasted no time, going immediately to the cash register and pulling out five hundred in tens, twenties, and fifties. She made sure to leave some of each so it wouldn't be immediately noticeable. As quickly as she could, she stashed it in the bottom of her backpack. Then, she continued to serve the few people who were coming in until Rosa got back. She excused herself to the bathroom, waited a few minutes, then came out and told Rosa she wasn't feeling well.

"Go home, sweetheart. It's ok. You helped so much with the

morning rush. I'll see you tomorrow if you're feeling better. If not, just come back when you feel good again." Rosa reached out and hugged Annabelle and sent her on her way. Annabelle grabbed her backpack and almost ran to the river. She was late.

As you approach the river and see Pedro pacing there, you wish again that you could ditch him. You'd so much rather spend your time with giving people like Rosa, who had probably discovered the theft by now. The book holds you hostage, though, and you're stuck. You just hope the five hundred puts Pedro in a better mood today.

"Here." You thrust the cash into his hand. "I found Caretaker. I'll make contact today and get inside. I'll get the schedule; we'll make the plan. And then you'll have all the high-end art you can fence."

"Hello to you too, sexy." Pedro flipped through the cash with an evil grin on his face.

"Hello and goodbye. I haven't slept in ages, and I'm beat. I'm going to go find a place to crash. I'll see you tomorrow." Annabelle waved goodbye over her shoulder as she walked away, not giving him a chance to argue or to follow her. Her two favorite sleeping places were taken, so she headed to the garden. The hidden place with the soft grass would work well as a place to crash for a few hours.

When you get to the garden, you find your neatly folded hoodie in the place where you had left the sleeping Comforter. You quickly curl up with your head on it and fall sound asleep without the help of alcohol.

CHAPTER 9

Chapter 6—Day 7, noon

As soon as you're asleep the dreams start. You've got a machete in your hand, and you're carrying a heavy load. You turn around slowly and see your Protector with tears in his eyes. Turning back, you begin making your way down the overgrown path. The work is slow and hard, and made harder by the burden on your back. When you reach a small clearing, you put down the burden and the knife and stretch your back. Turning, you see someone crumpled over. They're sobbing their heart out. When you get closer, you see that it's Rosa. There is suddenly a large wad of cash in your hand, and it's burning into your palm. You drop it and run back the way you had come, forgetting all about the machete and the load you were carrying. You run past your Protector and then past your Caretaker. As you run you look at your burning *palm and see the white mark has turned black. You see the statue of the cow ahead and run toward it as fast as you can, but it seems to be getting further and further away.*

You wake up from your restless sleep to the sound of a mother calling her young kids to come home for lunch. It wasn't enough sleep, but it'll have to do. You've got a lot to do! You throw your hoodie in your backpack, pull out the ankle brace, and stash the backpack as far back in the bushes as you can. Then, you head to the gas station, where you left the wheelchair. Thankfully, it's still where you left it, and it hasn't rained or anything to make a mess of things. You pull it out and go back toward the garden. Once you get close, you settle into the wheelchair and put the brace on your left ankle. You've always had great upper body strength, and thankfully, this time, the roads are relatively flat. It doesn't take long to find the street you followed Caretaker to last night. You take a moment to get your story straight and regulate your breathing before you navigate up to the Caretaker's front door. On your way, you can't help but move the wind chime. The sound is subtle and pleasant and makes you smile.

Annabelle looked through the window in the front door and saw a homey living room. The furniture all looked well-worn and comfortable. The walls were brightly colored the way Caretaker's always were. It had to be the right place. With one more deep breath, she knocked on the door.

You wait what seems like an eternity for Caretaker to come into view. She looks younger than you've ever seen her. The two of you look more like contemporaries than Caretaker and Charge.

Annabelle watched Caretaker's face as she opened the door. As a flash of recognition enters her eyes, three streaks of gray cascade down her hair. The crinkles on the side of her eyes grow deeper. The smile she gives you is forced, but Annabelle noted with relief that it was still a smile. Just in time, she remembered to smile in return.

"Annabelle!" Caretaker cast about for words, "How did you...? That is, I didn't expect... what a lovely surprise! But what has happened to your ankle?"

Annabelle couldn't place the emotions bubbling around inside her gut so she stopped trying to give them a name and instead got her head back into today's pressing problems.

A couple more strands of gray framed Caretaker's face by the time Annabelle had finished her story. She leaned wearily on the door frame. "Well, come on in. Would you like some coffee? I was just about to make some. And then you can tell me what you're looking for, and we'll see if I can help you."

Annabelle wondered why she could see Caretaker aging in front of her eyes, but she didn't think about it for too long. It was working, that's all that mattered. In no time she'd be rolling through that gate and have a chance to figure out when the shipment headed for the other side of the island. "Thank you, Caretaker!" And she rolled inside.

Annabelle looked around as they went through the living room and dining room into the kitchen. The house was much smaller than when she had lived with Caretaker, but everything still felt familiar and homey. "This is such a great little house! I know I never lived here, but it almost feels like I was never gone!"

"I'm glad you like it." Caretaker handed her a steaming mug of coffee and picked one up for herself. She leaned back against the countertop, looking comfortable and decidedly *un*comfortable at the same time.

"So, do you have any kids now? This feels smaller?"

"There is only one left, and he won't be here for long," Caretaker replied, sipping at the coffee. "Why don't you tell me how I can help you out with your sprained ankle and your new job?"

"Oh! Yes! Well, um, it's like this. Before I got the new job I was spending a lot of time in the Keeper's garden. I was in a tough spot, and I remembered how you always told me to get close to the Keeper, ya know, and things would get better. But they didn't, at least for a while. So I just kept at it. I went every day after working the docks. But you know how the docks are full of pretty bad people, so it was hard to keep going. But I did it!" Annabelle looked up with a hopeful smile and wide blueish eyes, expecting to see Caretaker's usual affirming smile. But Caretaker was looking down into her coffee for all the world as if there were something terribly interesting happening inside the mug. The only sign she was listening was her quiet "mmm" of assent.

"Anyway, when I was spending all that time in the garden I got to see a lot of people going in and out through the gate. And one time, I watched a young man go in with a woman. She took him inside. When they walked in, he was limping, but when they came out, he was healed.

"Ahhh, I see," Caretaker said with a lift of her eyebrows. "You're talking about the Writer's room."

"Um, yes," Annabelle answered quickly, even as her mind whirled with the new information. "I don't have anyone else in my life that I can go to for help."

"What about Pedro?" Caretaker was suddenly intensely focused on Annabelle's face.

Annabelle shifted her face to one that looked appropriately sadder and wiser. "He was no good for me." *That much is true anyway.* "He kept pulling me into all the things you warned me not to do. I had to break up with him. That was over a year ago; I haven't seen him since.

82

Besides, he never would have helped me get into the Writer's room; he hated the Writer." *Also true.*

"Well, if that's true, it was a good decision." Caretaker looked skeptical at best.

Annabelle decided to press on instead of dwelling on Pedro. "Like I was saying, I don't have anyone to help me. And with this wheelchair I can't get in through the gate and down the stairs on my own. Would you be able to help me? I believe that I would find healing there for my ankle, and I would be able to go back to work." Annabelle put on her most sincere and innocent face. "I was going to wait to see you until I had saved up enough money for my own place so I could show you! I was getting close, but this sprained ankle set me back! I had doctor's bills and a wheelchair rental to pay. I've been saving bit by bit, trying to earn my way."

When Annabelle looked up she thought she caught the tail end of an eye roll from Caretaker, but she couldn't be sure. Caretaker covered it quickly with another sip of her coffee.

"I'd be happy to take you to the Writer's room, Annabelle." Caretaker took a final sip and set her coffee mug on the counter behind her. "In fact, you're often on my mind when I'm there. Is now a good time for you? I have time."

Annabelle had barely touched her coffee, so she quickly sipped and followed suit. "Yes, of course! I'd love to get back to work as soon as I can. I don't like dipping into my savings."

"Just let me get my shoes on, and we can go. I'm sure you know it's not far from here."

Caretaker puts her shoes on and helps push you out the door and down the drive to the street. When you turn onto the main street, you see a tall young man in a uniform headed your way. His curly hair gives him away: The Watcher! You wince at the thought of an inevitable meeting, and do some fast thinking for how to explain everything if he asks.

"Annabelle! Liev and I have been worried about you ever since he fell asleep in the garden and you disappeared! Man, he's going to be so glad to hear you're ok! But, actually," Adler looked down at her ankle, "Are you ok? What happened?"

"Oh, you know, I actually got a job at Rosa's, and I was running an errand for her, and I tripped. Caused all sorts of trouble with my ankle." Annabelle gestured to Caretaker, who was looking on with interest, "This is my Caretaker; she's been kind enough to take me on a walk to the garden today. You know how I love being there, close to the Keeper and all."

"Is that why you're always there?" The look on Adler's face was doubtful, but he shrugged in his happy way and smiled at her, "Have a nice walk, ladies. It's a beautiful day." Then he winked at Caretaker, who wore a knowing grin and meandered on his way.

"Charming young man, seems like you could've asked him for some help?" Caretaker queried.

Annabelle scrambled for an excuse, "Oh, you know, he's one of the Keeper's agents. He's very busy. I couldn't bother him."

"Annabelle," Caretaker paused for a moment, "why do you really want to get into the Writer's room?"

"Rosa is counting on me, and I'm counting on myself to keep this job. It's very important to me. You'd like Rosa. She's sweet and funny, and she's very giving. She... she kinda reminds me of you."

Caretaker was quiet for the rest of the trip to the garden and the gate Annabelle couldn't wait to get through. The excitement was building inside of her. Finally, her plan was in action. In just a little while, she would have the schedule, and then she could get across to the other side of the island. And then she'd be free—free to write her *own* story.

They arrived at the gate, and Caretaker stopped pushing the wheelchair and waited. After a moment, Annabelle became confused.

"Is… is everything ok?"

"Sure! It's great. Why?" Caretaker responded in a carefree tone.

"You stopped. I thought you were going to help me through the gate." Annabelle noticed the hint of petulance in her voice. She hoped Caretaker hadn't heard it.

"Annabelle, darling, wave your hand so the gate will open. Then I can push you through it and down the stairs."

Annabelle whipped her head around to look at Caretaker's face. *Oh, Keeper, what do I do now?*

"I can't reach the sensor. Can't you do it?" Annabelle stopped just shy of saying she'd seen Caretaker go in before. She didn't like the look on Caretaker's face. It was almost other-worldly. Her face was covered in a calm that worked its way under Annabelle's skin and made her insides roll.

"The Writer would never let his room be inaccessible to anyone. Just lift your hand and hold it palm toward the gate." Caretaker folded her own hands at her waist and simply waited. Annabelle's mind froze as she stared at the white mark on her palm. She slowly lifted her hand toward the gate. Just like before, nothing happened.

"Annabelle." Caretaker's voice was firm and unyielding. "You don't know what your mark is for yet, do you." It wasn't a question. Caretaker thought for just a moment, then seemed to have made a decision. "I'm going to leave you here in the garden since you like it so well. There's a nice spot over there by the wall." She maneuvered the wheelchair over to the place where Annabelle had spent her days. "When you've learned what it means, come back and see me. I'll take you down to the Writer's room anytime. But remember what I told you about the mark."

Annabelle turned her head toward Caretaker and yelled, "You don't care. You never cared. If you cared, you would let me into that room. You know how to get in there, I know you do. All I want is to get back to my job. All I want is for you to help me with this one small thing. You said the Writer would never keep anyone out of his room. But he's keeping me from entering, and you're helping him! You care more about him than about me, and you were my Caretaker! Pedro was right all along. He told me you didn't care about me, and he was *right!*" With this, Annabelle broke into loud sobs.

Caretaker looked at her for just a moment, then said with deadly calm, "It isn't the Writer who is keeping you from entering the gate. It's you." With that, Caretaker walked back to the gate, lifted her hand, and entered through the gate. Her hair had gone completely silver, and she walked as if a weight had been placed on her. From the hand she raised, Annabelle knew it was the same white mark that she had on hers. It didn't make any sense!

All the hope left Annabelle. She would never get that schedule. And in 5 days, she would die. *I'll die sooner if I don't get that schedule.* Pedro is expecting it by tomorrow morning. I'm screwed. Her hope-lessness grew and alongside it, her rage against Caretaker. Since there was no way into the gate anymore, she was stuck going back to the first plan—breaking into the back door. She dug around behind her back and found her shoe. Then she took off the ankle brace, put on her shoe, and hid the wheelchair in the back alley. Just then, she saw both of the Keeper's agents turn into the alley, so she ducked back into the shadows.

Liev was talking to Adler. "I'm telling you, this one is a tough cookie. You think you're starting to get through to her, but she starts to get a little soft, and then all of a sudden, she's lying to your face. Eyes wide open, staring straight into yours, she tells you a flat lie! Imagine saying she fell and sprained her ankle when really she stole all that money. You should have seen Rosa today; she was devastated. It's gonna take more than a story to lift her up this time." The Comforter was shaking his head and looking at the ground, shoulders slumped.

"Cheer up, Liev," Adler threw his arm around Liev's shoulder. "The messenger wouldn't have sent both of us without a good reason. There's gotta be hope in there, somewhere. You can't give up on her yet. Your job isn't done, and neither is mine. We just have to keep on going." Apparently, it was the Watcher's turn to do the comforting.

"Easy for you to say, you know what your job is!" Liev shoved Adler away playfully.

Adler snorted, "You're kidding, right? You think it's going to be easy to get that kid to open up communication with the Messenger?!? She's shut down the last few messages, and you know how hard it is to turn that train around!"

Liev shot back at him, "I know she wouldn't read the message! That was the one that explained why on earth I had to be there! Now, I'm just fumbling around in the dark, trying to figure out what the purpose is. And on top of that, I'm stuck trying to figure it out with a person who couldn't find the truth with two hands and a flashlight."

"Well, we've both got our work cut out for us with this one. But the Keeper must see something in Annabelle that makes it worth it." Adler shrugged, and they both turned toward the back door of the Keeper's court. "Anyway, we aren't on Annabelle duty until later tonight. Let's go check the rest of the schedule and see if there's anything coming up that can take our mind off it for a little while. Whadduya say?"

Liev pulled a key ring from his pocket and located the key he was looking for. "Sure, let's do that. Hey, thanks for..." His voice moved out of hearing and the door hit the frame and rested there until someone from the inside pulled it fully shut.

You stand up and realize your foot is asleep, so you wiggle your toes and wait a moment before you head out. You know everything you need to know now. The Comforter has the key to the back door and he's assigned to you later that night. You'll find him in the garden later and when he falls asleep again, and you'll take the keys. And the schedule is somewhere behind that door, just like you suspected. If all goes well, you'll have the information you need before the morning, after all.

CHAPTER 10

Chapter 6—Day 8, midnight
The Comforter and The Watcher are waiting for you
behind the bushes. You see a flash of the gold emblem on
one of their uniforms as you walk up. Aside from the
seals, the green of the uniforms camouflages them nicely.
You greet them cheerfully, which throws them off their
game just a little bit. But they recover quickly and settle
into the conversation.

"Hey, fellas, you almost blend in back here. Having a midnight picnic?" Annabelle gestures to the bag of snacks they had apparently brought with them tonight.

"We knew you'd be back, and we also knew it would be a long night. We had other duties today to take care of and only short naps. So! Food it is. Would you like some?" Liev held the bag up for Annabelle to inspect. They had gone all out in their preparation, and she quickly selected a chocolate bar and some gummy worms. Then she crossed her ankles and, in one movement, sat down with crossed legs.

"So what's the plan tonight, guys? My work here is done, but I couldn't resist another night in your swell company. Besides, I did have a nice long nap today down by the river. I'm wide awake." As she asked, Annabelle opened the chocolate bar and took a bite, savoring the rich flavor.

"Uh, plan. What's the plan... We don't have a plan. Do we? Liev?" Adler looked bewildered by the change in Annabelle's demeanor.

Liev looked just as confused, "Um, no. No plan. Just orders to be here, really. What do you mean your job here is done? What was it?"

Annabelle raised one shoulder, tipped her head toward it, and answered him in a cheerful tone, "Oh well, ya know, it doesn't really matter. It didn't work out anyway." She pulled her Future Book out of her bag and held it up. "This thing is just the worst. Do you ever feel like nothing ever works out? Like no matter how hard you try, you're doomed to keep repeating the same story over and over?"

"*What happened?* Your Future book looks like it's been set on fire and dumped in the river and then run over by a truck!" Adler laughed in shock and disbelief.

"Well, you're wrong about the truck. And it was a fountain, not a river. But otherwise, you're spot on." Annabelle dropped it on the grass next to her, and Liev picked it up and examined the cracked leather.

"May I? I've never actually seen the inside of a Future book before." He looked over to her eagerly. "I promise I'll only read a page or two, and you can choose the pages!"

"Like I care. Read whatever you want. There's a super intense ending if you like that sort of thing. Read away!" It hadn't been her intent to let them see any of her Future Book; she didn't know why she did. Suddenly, she had an alarming thought, "Oh, but maybe stay away from the last chapter other than the last couple of pages, ok? It's kinda weird having you know what I'm thinking while I'm thinking it."

Liev nodded in agreement and excitedly flipped open the book to an early page and began reading. While he did, Adler began asking questions.

"You're on your last chapter?"

He genuinely looks concerned. "Yes, I'm getting close to the end, too." Annabelle looked down at the bag of gummy worms, avoiding his sympathetic eyes and pushing away thoughts of the final day.

"Is it weird to know everything before it happens? Like, what's that like? How do you deal with knowing the end is coming close, especially since you don't have the messages to comfort you? I don't know what I would do."

"What do you mean, 'what's that like'? Don't you have a Future book? Wait, Liev hasn't ever read one; that must mean he doesn't have one either?"

"Nah, we don't get one. We were chosen very young to be agents for the Keeper. I guess he figured we don't need one since we have pretty specific tasks to carry out each day anyway. Knowing our future would just get in the way of what needs to be done now, don't you think? We'd always be thinking about tomorrow instead of today, and today has enough to do and think about!"

Annabelle couldn't imagine a life without her Future Book. As much as she hated it, it did give her a constant—something that was predictable and secure.

"Hey!" Liev looked up from his reading, "Who's Conrad?"

"Oh. Keeper." Annabelle rolled her eyes. "That's my kid brother."

"He sounds fun. In this part, he's standing on a tree stump, giving you an air guitar concert while you jump in some leaves. But you don't seem to care for it or him too much. OR the leaves. You keep throwing out fake smiles and hollow laughter. What's the story there?"

"You're reading the Future book. You're like, inside my head! You should be able to see what's going on."

Liev chose another spot in the book a little further on and went back to his reading. Annabelle picked up a piece of grass and started splitting it with her chewed-off fingernails. Adler just sat and watched the two of them. After a while, Liev began laughing.

Annabelle tried to snatch the book out of his hand, but he held it away from her.

"What are you laughing at?" She growled at him.

Liev continued to laugh, that hiccup-like laugh that made him seem so much younger. "You tell the worst dad jokes ever! You *and* your Protector. These are horrible." He could barely get the words out through the laughter.

Annabelle smiled at the memory and picked up another blade of grass to demolish.

Liev flipped to the back of the book. After a moment, he handed the book back to her. His brow was furrowed. To Annabelle, he seemed very worried.

"I know. It's a horrible ending. That's why the book was burned and water-damaged. When I was finally able to read it I was so mad I threw it into the fire and into a fountain. But it didn't do any good. Nothing has done any good in changing what happens. I'm stuck."

"Um, Annabelle? Are you...? I was just..." Liev noticed Adler, who was frantically swiping a finger across his throat and stopped mid-sentence. "What?!?"

Adler looked from Liev to Annabelle and back again. "There's a time to talk and a time to be silent. This is one of those silent times."

"But.."

"No." Adler stared Liev down. For once, Liev took the hint and looked away, his eyebrows still knit together.

Annabelle messed with the page edges before she put the book back in her backpack. She was angry with herself. Why did she let him read her book? She hadn't thought of Conrad in ages, and she didn't want to think about him now. He was a teenager when she left, and she hadn't talked to him since. He was all grown up now and doing just fine without her. He hadn't ever tried to find her—probably forgot she existed.

You lie back on the grass and look up at the stars

through the trees. Next to you, you hear the two young men do the same. You try to shift your focus back to the present. After all, you're on an urgent mission—a mission of life and death. YOUR death. The quiet presence of the Keeper's agents calms the tumultuous emotions swirling around inside your head. You feel yourself begin to drift, so you dig your short fingernails into the palm of your hand. You must stay awake if you're going to complete your mission tonight! But the dancing leaves above your head, and the stars that dart in and out all begin to fade as you shift between waking and sleeping. It's not too long before you're dreaming again.

Annabelle ran back toward the gate in the cow statue, but as she got closer, she saw a tall, muscled man with arms crossed and feet spread wide standing in front of it. His hair was dark and wavy, and his jaw was square and strong. Just as she began to think he looked familiar, she saw a picture of a young boy with feet spread wide, wildly playing air guitar. The boy was missing teeth and wearing thick glasses. She looked up at the man's face and saw the glasses were there, but now they seemed to suit him well. It was Conrad, all grown up, but he didn't look happy.

"You have to turn around," he said as she approached. His voice was deep and self-assured.

"Conrad! Conrad, it's been so long! You've grown!"

"You have to turn around," he repeated.

"I don't want to turn around. It's too hard that way. There are too many expectations and too many people I've hurt. Please, I want to get out of here. Open the gate." Annabelle whined to Conrad.

"Annabelle, you have to turn around. The only way forward is back. You have a chance, and the truth will set you free. Don't waste it." His face was stern and unmoving, but behind his eyes were the hurt ones of a little boy.

"Conrad, come with me. We can go through the gate and escape this place.

We can start a new life and forget all about the old one. We can do it together. I just need your help to get through the gate. Then we'll head for the mainland! We'll make a good life." Annabelle pleaded with him, hoping to reach the little boy inside who always longed for adventure and new horizons.

A tear slipped down his cheek, but his face never faltered. "The only way for you to be free is to carry on to the end of the path. I'll meet you on the other side."

"At least come with me! I can't do this. It's too hard." Annabelle tried tears.

"No. No one can do this for you. It's your path." With that, he turned his back to her, still standing in front of the gate.

She woke up to Adler and Liev whispering furiously. "That's what I'm telling you, Adler; there was nothing there!"

"Should you say something?" Adler asked, then noticed Annabelle had woken up. "Hello, sleepyhead! Have a nice nap?"

"Uggghh. No. It was not a nice nap. How long did I sleep?" Annabelle rubbed her eyes as she sat up next to the agents.

"Don't worry, it wasn't long," Liev answered her. "So, anyway, Annabelle, something came up while you were asleep, and we've got to go. We were really just waiting til you woke up."

"What do you mean, something came up? How did something come up here in the garden in the middle of the night?" Annabelle was more worried about her plan than confused, but she played up the confusion. Anything to keep them there longer.

Adler answered her, "The messenger came by. I hate to sound like a broken record, but you've got a message, too." He nodded toward an envelope on the grass next to her hand. "You may want to try reading it this time?" His eyebrows were raised suggestively, and his eyes were sparkling again.

Annabelle picked up the envelope and toyed with it for a moment, trying to decide what to do. If she opened it, the agents may stick around for a while. She could pretend she really wanted to hear from the messenger. That would keep Adler there, ready to work with her, she was certain. But, he might not believe such a sudden change of heart either. Liev might be the better play. Or, she could let them both go. She was tired of the work it took to stay on their good side, and she was tired of pretending to be ok. She angrily made her choice, staring up at Adler and Liev and deliberately dropping the envelope back on the grass. She let the hatred spill out of her eyes for just a moment, just long enough for them to see it. Then she ducked her head down again and said, "bye."

You hear the heavy sighs of the agents before they move to go. You're inclined to sigh heavily yourself. There's no way to get in that back door now except going back to the very first idea— breaking in. You gather yourself together. Breaking in really isn't your strength, and you hate the thought that you might get caught, but you don't see any other options left to you. A movement at the gate catches your eye. A young woman with a ponytail walks out. You look more closely and see that it's Caretaker. You're not quite sure what time it is because of your nap, but the sky is beginning to show signs of morning. You know Caretaker has been in there for at least half a day by now. She had walked in there, an old woman, the day before. The sound of her singing wafts across the garden. You can almost feel it reflect off the metallic hardness inside of you. Her youth and joy serve as reminders that you mean nothing to her. She could have helped you if she cared. Anger fuels you, and before you know it, you're storming across the garden toward Caretaker.

What am I doing!?! Annabelle screamed inside her head, but it was too late. Caretaker had already noticed her and was clearly waiting for her approach. The singing stopped.

"How dare you? How dare you leave me in this garden and go inside the gate when you knew I needed to get back there? Don't you care about me at all? You clearly know how to get inside the gate and I clearly don't. I *need* your help. It's your job to care about me and what matters to me. You're not being a good caretaker. You're failing! How do they even let you be a caretaker? Or maybe that's why it's your last kid leaving. Because you don't deserve to be a caretaker anymore. Maybe you got fired because of how you're treating me, how you've always treated me. I bet none of the rest of the kids in your care felt loved, either. Even if they say they do, they are just faking it, so you'll give them stuff." Annabelle fully expected the force of her tirade to transform Caretaker back into the old version of herself, but it didn't seem to phase her at all. She just stood there, smiling.

"Annabelle, if you want to go in the gate, I'll take you." She laughed, "But clearly, it's not to get healing for your ankle? Do you want to tell me why you want to get in there so desperately?"

Annabelle stopped just a moment in shock and looked down at her ankle. *Oops.* "Why would I tell you that? Why would I trust you with anything?"

Caretaker nodded once. "Ok. Well, I have instructions to take you into the Writer's room. Do you still want me to take you in?"

"Yes."

CHAPTER 11

Chapter 6—Day 8, early dawn

Caretaker almost bounces to the gate, completely contra-dicting the seriousness of just a moment before. She tells you joyfully that this is her favorite place on earth. And she waves her hand near the symbol of the four crea-tures. The sound of the latch opening makes your breath catch in your throat. You're hesitant now to enter, but Caretaker is pulling the gate open and walking down the stairs to the door. You follow suit and the door swings open as you approach it together. The door looked normal size to you, but you find you have to duck as you enter.

Annabelle looked around the comfortably lit room. It seemed like an old attic—wood walls, floor and ceiling. The ceiling was slanted on both sides, with a small window at the end letting in full daylight. The only other source of light was a single bulb that hung from the ceiling with a pull string, but she could see everything clearly. There were drawings and writing all over the floor, the ceiling and the walls. She saw in a flash that her name had been written in several places, but the rest of the writing was unclear to her. She began to look at the furnishings. Nearest to her, there was an old frayed couch. Across from that, there was a wooden rocking chair and an overstuffed, oversized recliner. On the far side of the room, there was a wooden railing surrounding stairs headed down.

"Why does this place look like an old attic?" Annabelle turned to ask Caretaker, who was engrossed in filling an empty section of wall. The question hung in the air for the time it took her to register that Annabelle was talking to her.

"I'm sorry, what did you say?" She asked, absentmindedly sticking her charcoal pencil into her ponytail.

"What is this place? Why does it look like an old attic?" Annabelle asked impatiently.

A voice as deep as the ocean and as soothing as its waves washed into the room from the corner with the stairs, "I can answer that."

Annabelle jumped. Caretaker smiled and turned to the source of the voice. The Writer stepped up into the room and smiled. The Writer had seemed small in comparison to the Keeper, but to Annabelle, now it seemed his presence filled the small attic room. She felt exposed as if her plan to get across to the other side of the island was laid bare in front of her. She took an involuntary step backward while Caretaker *leaped* into his arms. The Writer's smile grew.

"Emory."

Annabelle realized with a flash she had never heard Caretaker's name before the Writer spoke it. That one word from the Writer's mouth seemed to convey an eternity of love and intimacy as he folded Caretaker into his arms. She looked more than *young*. She glowed. Annabelle felt small and mean in comparison as if her presence was an imposition. But when Caretaker moved away from the embrace and began her industrious writing again, the Writer shifted his focus to Annabelle. He held out an arm to her in an invitation, but she couldn't fling herself into his arms the way Caretaker did. She knew she had to acknowledge it in some way though, so she tentatively held out her hand to shake his. When he said her name and his hand touched hers she felt a fire inside of her, as if it were burning away parts of her. She pulled back quickly.

"So, uh, Writer, why is this room like an old attic?" She stammered out the question, not caring anymore about the answer but wanting his eyes to look at anything but her. He looked right into her, and she felt an uncomfortable awareness of her true self. His eyes commanded attention, and she barely noticed anything else about him.

You don't even listen to the answer as he speaks in a golden voice and gestures to different parts of the room and to Caretaker. You just nod along. All you can think about is how to get out of the room you wanted so desperately to get inside of! You zone back in just in time to hear him speak again.

"But, please, have a seat. You look uncomfortable, but this room is designed for comfort." The Writer sat back on one side of the couch and gestured to the other open spaces. That was the last thing Annabelle wanted, to sit and have a chat with the Writer in this oppressively small and intimate space. Nevertheless, she sat. It was really more of a perch. She perched on the edge of the recliner, feeling like she may bolt at any moment. The Writer laughed, and the sound of his laughter filled the room. To Annabelle, it seemed like the room grew brighter and warmer at the sound. "I'm not going to eat you. But I am going to ask you a question."

Annabelle felt her ears grow hot. "Um, o-okay."

"Why aren't you reading my notes?" The Writer pointed to a stack of black envelopes that appeared in her lap.

Annabelle jumped, scattering the envelopes across the floor. Then, she quickly fell to her knees and began gathering the stack. When she had them all, she regained her perch and placed them on the arm of the chair.

"Sorry. That surprised me." She grinned over to the Writer. "It reminds me of the time that…"

"That your brother did the thing with the fishing wire and the rubber snake. I know." The Writer cut her off. "But that doesn't answer my question."

"What was the question?" She remembered, but she needed more time to think of a plausible excuse.

"Why aren't you reading my notes?" He asked the question gently and without any anger. She looked into his eyes for just a moment but found she couldn't maintain the gaze.

"I didn't know they were yours." Annabelle inwardly cringed. *That was weak.*

"You did." His reply was simple.

"Okay, maybe. But there was nothing there on the last one I read, anyway. I don't know why. But, um, I really need to go. Today is kinda important, and I've got a lot to do."

"Like breaking into the back door. I've already taken care of that for you. I left it ever so slightly ajar. You'll be able to walk right in." He maintained steady eye contact.

"What?" Annabelle stared at him. Terror filled her at his first word, and then a chaotic confusion followed. "Why?!?"

"It's easier. This way, I don't have to have the locks replaced." His deep brown eyes were twinkling at her, but all Annabelle could do was blink. "Now, listen, take the notes with you. I've written copies of the old ones, plus I've added a few more. You're going to need them soon, so don't lose them!"

Annabelle absently picked up the envelopes and stood to go. Caretaker left her writing and drawing and came close. "Goodbye, Annabelle. I hope you figure it all out soon." She smiled sadly at her. "And, when you do, come and see me again. I've missed you." Caretaker started to reach her hands out as if to offer an embrace but thought better of it and waved instead.

Annabelle waved in return and left the way they had come in. As she turned to let the door close slowly, she saw Caretaker flop on the couch next to the Writer. He was saying something Annabelle couldn't hear, and Caretaker smiled up at him. Then the door closed and hid them from view. Annabelle jetted up the steps, through the gate, and back to her hiding place in the bushes and trees.

Did that just happen? She shook her head and realized she was shaking all over. She thrust the envelopes into her backpack and laid back down on the soft grass. The sun was fully up now, but the spot she had chosen was shaded and cool. As her breathing slowed and the shaking stopped, it dawned on her that the sun being fully up meant her time was up. She *had* to get into that room, and now.

The door is open. If... if I can trust what the Writer said to me. But why would he leave it open for me? What if it is open but there's someone behind it waiting to take me away? How can I walk in there? The thought terrified her, now more than ever. Before, the plan had been to break in during the night when no one was around. Now, she was supposed to just walk in in broad daylight? She looked down at her clothes and realized there was no way she would blend in with what she was wearing. Her mind went to the uniform she had stashed by the river. But Pedro was no doubt already there, waiting for her. If she showed up without the schedule there was no knowing what he would do. And if she got caught in her fake uniform she wouldn't be able to use it on an actual day. No, she couldn't go get her uniform. She would have to just take her chances on the door with what she was wearing. But she did throw on her hoodie.

It is, quite literally, now or never. You stand up and take a deep breath. Leaving your backpack tucked away in the bushes, you make your way to the back door. It is exactly how the Writer said it would be—very slightly ajar. It creaks as you slowly open it, and you pause to listen. For the moment, it seems like everything is clear. You finish opening the door just wide enough to slip through and let it shut behind you. You find yourself in a brightly lit hallway with several doors on either side.

Each of the doors is different—different colors, different styles, even different materials. With nothing to indicate what might be behind them, finding the schedule for the truck may take all day.

A noise down the hallway startled Annabelle. For half a second, she felt frozen in place, then she jumped to the nearest door, a wood door with many embellishments and all painted yellow, and ducked inside, but when she looked around, she found she wasn't in a room at all. The only room-like thing that remained was the door. Everything else had vanished, and in its place, there was a field of grain that continued past the horizon. The sun shone brightly overhead in a pure blue sky. The air felt fresh and clear. Annabelle breathed in deeply and released the stress of the past few hours. She felt as if her energy had been restored and, with it, clear thought. Without a second thought, she spun through the rows. She sat and then laid in between a couple of rows of grain and almost giggled out loud. She flung her arms over her head and closed her eyes. She wished she could stay here forever, but she had to keep searching. Annabelle groaned and rolled over to stand.

You turn back to the door and crack it open. Listening shows you there's no more noise in the hallway, so you slide through the door and slowly guide the door closed. You decide to go through the hallway, checking all the doors on the left first, so you go to the next one. This door is made of actual gold and covered in jewels. You open the door and sneak through. The lights are lower here, so it takes a moment for your eyes to adjust. When they do, you discover that you're looking down on a labyrinth of shelves completely overrun with rolled-up scrolls. Unlike the open fields, the air in here is stuffy and dry. You fight the urge to bolt from the room, but you still push past the door without looking for anyone in the hallway. Once you emerge, you gasp for air.

Two doors down, only twenty or so to go. Annabelle dreaded whatever was behind the next door. The door itself was covered in an astounding mosaic of tiles depicting a garden scene. When she opened it and poked her head inside, she found the purest white walls towering high above her. In between them, there were again rows of shelves. Impatient, she pulled back into the hallway and let the door close.

Annabelle was starting to wonder if she was even looking in the right hallway. None of these rooms seemed to be office-like in the least! The despair of futility clawed at her throat, but she kept going. The next door didn't feel like it could possibly be right. It was made of ancient wood, splitting from age. Random rusty nails poked out of it. Annabelle skipped that door in favor of the next one, which was covered in vines, the gold handle barely visible between the leaves. She opened the door and peeked inside. The light was blinding for a moment, and then she saw that it was again the sunshine magnified by the reflection off miles and miles of sandy dunes. She didn't even bother to step inside.

Moving on, she found a simple door. Aside from the purple color, there was nothing extraordinary about it. No additional decorations or embellishments. She opened the door and walked into what appeared to be a cozy office. The lighting was muted but clear. The calm and order of the room steadied Annabelle's spirits. She looked around for the likeliest spot and found a bookshelf with several binders on one of the shelves. One that said, "Alternate Endings" caught her attention. She pulled it out and opened the first page, finding a list of names. She flipped through and saw the list was extensive. Behind each name, there was a corresponding file number. She wondered if her name was in there and where the files were kept. A noise in the hallway made her heart skip a beat. She put the binder back and searched the other binders. Reading the labels quickly revealed that one of them contained shipping schedules. She removed it from the shelf and flipped through, finding all manner of shipments coming in and going out. Finally, she landed on the one she was looking for. Her heart quickened. Future Books to Canree Nu East, Delivered by: Watcher and Comforter. And then the date.

She had what she needed. She hastily closed the binder and replaced it on the shelf. She practically ran out the door and down the hallway to the exit. Emerging from the building into the alley revealed that storm clouds had moved in. They threatened to drop their load at any time. Annabelle threw her hood over her head and bolted to the hiding spot in the bushes. She grabbed her backpack and took off for her spot by the river, wondering if she would be drenched by the time she got there. Having the information she needed for the next step made her feel lighter than air. As she ran toward the dock, she leaped and spun. The heavens opened up, and the rain fell in a torrential downpour, but she didn't care. She spread her arms wide and spun around again, lifting her face to the sky.

You slow down as you approach the river. No sense in letting Pedro know you're happy. He will do everything he can to destroy that feeling for you. Better to look miserable and angry. You scan the riverbank for a sign of Pedro, but you don't see him. A quick search reveals he's nowhere in the vicinity. You duck under the bridge and find your chair to wait for him to come back, thinking maybe the rain scared him away. You're not sad, though. You take a few more moments to celebrate the success of your trip inside the back halls of the Keeper's court. You rest your head against the back of the chair and sigh happily.

"You sound awfully happy for a person who was supposed to be here an hour ago with my information." Pedro's voice was ominous. Annabelle could have given him the good news right away, but she couldn't resist the urge to mess with him first.

"Did you bring breakfast? I'm starving."

"Are you kidding me? I was here waiting forever, and then I got hungry. I remembered that amazing cinnamon roll and headed to Rosa's for some food. The whole place was shut down and boarded up. So, no. No food for me. And definitely no food for you. You want something to eat, go get it yourself." No wonder he was surly, he hadn't eaten.

"Oh, ok, I'll go grab some food then I'll be back." She knew he wouldn't let her go but she took a couple steps like she was going to leave. He lunged toward her and grabbed her arm.

"No, no, Chiquita. First, you're going to tell me what I need to know." His grip tightened, and Annabelle winced.

"What you need to know is that I'm hungry, and I'm going to get food." She shot back at him.

"Are you telling me you don't know when the shipment goes over to the other island? That's going to cost you a lot more than a measly 500." He pulled her toward him.

She stared straight into his eyes without blinking. "Relax. I know when the shipment leaves. And I know who's driving it."

CHAPTER 12

Chapter 6—Day 9

You open one eye slowly and groan. Your head is throbbing. Every sound sets off a cascade of piercing echos in your brain. Even with the overcast sky, the light is too intense, and you slide your eyes shut again. After a moment, what you saw registers in your mind. You're back in your box, but you're not in any normal position. You must be curled up sideways in the fetal position at the foot of your box. You hadn't even bothered to pull out the sleeping bag last night, apparently. The cardboard-covered cement under you makes your hip ache. The strange position and the hangover have you feeling disoriented. You're completely unaware of the time of day. You open one bleary eye again and notice your backpack is in the corner of your box. You don't remember putting it there. In fact, you don't remember the night before at all.

The sound of voices nearby pulls you into a painfully alert state.

"The Messenger said we would find her here and that our time is running out. She's gotta be in one of these." From the sounds, the source of the voice was moving through the boxes, knocking on each one gently. Annabelle frowned, trying to place the voice. She knew she had heard it somewhere before.

"What does she mean that our time is running out? How can it be running out, there's nothing…" the first voice cut into the thought.

"I know. I don't understand it all, but it's what we've got to work with. She needs to read those notes before it's too late!" Understanding dawned on Annabelle. It was the Watcher and the Comforter coming looking for her, and apparently, they were on a mission. The knocking and footsteps grew closer and closer until the wall of her box shook ever so slightly with the Watcher's knock.

"Do you have to be so loud?" The sound of her own voice made her cringe, and she held out a hand as if to make herself quiet.

"Annabelle!" Both voices cried out together. Her first thought was to kill them for being so loud. Her second was, *How could they still be so happy to see me?*

A disheveled Annabelle stuck her head out the entrance to her box with her eyes as close to closed as she could get them. "What on earth do you two lunatics want so early in the morning?" She grumbled up a them.

Liev's jaw fell open a second before he burst into laughter. Adler just grinned and shook his head dramatically and gently said, "Oh my, Annabelle. You are a sight. You may want to find a hair brush and a fresh set of clothes before we go."

"I'm not going anywhere until you stop shouting and Liev stops cackling." She scowled at him, then disappeared inside the box to do exactly what he suggested.

You dig around until you find your hairbrush and

begin working out the tangles. While you do, you wonder why on earth you're going with them—and where you're going. A particularly nasty knot catches on the brush and makes you want to cry. You hear the men chatting quietly outside, but it's so quiet you can't make out the words. Once your hair is brushed and pulled back in a sleek ponytail, you search for a fresh outfit, eventually finding some joggers and a T-shirt.

Annabelle located her brush quickly and started yanking at her hair with it, listening to Liev and Adler chatting quietly about the weather. Every pull of the brush made her wince but when she reached the end and put her hair into its ponytail she noticed there wasn't one particular knot that caused her trouble. She threw on her favorite jeans and t-shirt and grabbed her backpack. She pushed out of the entrance but stopped short halfway out of her box. *This can't be right.*

Liev looked down at her in confusion, "Did you forget how to stand up? Need some help?" He held out his hand to her. When she didn't make any move to take it, he waved it in front of her face. "Hello? Annabelle?"

The sound of her name worked its way through the fog and she blinked and looked up at the hand Liev was once again holding out to her. She reached up to grab it, resolving to go back later and look at the Future book. Her memory must be slipping. It was probably time to refresh herself on it! She stood with Liev's help, then shrunk back down ever so slightly, shading her eyes with her hand. "Either of you guys have a pair of sunglasses I could borrow?"

Adler felt his pockets with no success, then pulled off his hat and held it out to her invitingly. "No sunglasses but could I offer you some shade?"

Annabelle took the hat and tried unsuccessfully to put it on her head. She had forgotten all about the ponytail. "Oh, I guess that's not going to work either." She handed the hat back to Adler.

"How about we go find a nice, quiet place for some breakfast and hot coffee?" Liev looked back and forth from Adler to Annabelle with one eyebrow raised in question.

"Sure. Sounds good. But you're buying." Annabelle grabbed for the arms of both guys at the same time, to steady herself and at the same time allow her to look downward, away from the sun, for the walk.

You walk right past Rosa's Cafe. From down the street, you can see the boards across the windows. You expect to feel bad about that, but you feel nothing. You did what you had to in order to survive; Rosa would just have to live with it. A few blocks later, you arrive at a corner diner.

"This place has the *best* coffee around," Liev patted her hand. "You'll be feeling better in no time."

He pulled open the door and Annabelle heard a bell ring. From behind the counter a short, dark-skinned woman with a small afro and caked on make-up pointed at a booth and called out, "Go ahead and grab a seat. I'll be there in a second," then turned back to the counter she was wiping down.

Liev and Adler scooted into the far side of the booth, and Annabelle slid halfway into the other side. They all flipped the coffee mugs upright, and almost instantly, the woman behind the counter was there with a brimming pot of coffee and three menus. She poured coffee into their cups and dropped the menus on the table in front of them, all with a disinterested and halfway disgusted attitude.

"I'll be back to take your orders." She spun around on one heel and trudged back behind the counter.

Annabelle picked up the coffee mug and brought it close, breathing in the bracing steam and taking a small sip. She burned her tongue but took another sip right away, then picked up the menu in front of her. When the server reappeared by their table, they were all ready to order.

Liev smiled up at her, "Good morning, Janae! Nice to see you again! How are things going with your nephew? Have you heard anything?"

Janae answered, "Six months, and we are no closer to a diagnosis. I think my sister has given up, but I'm still doing everything I can. Now. What can I get you today?" All of this was delivered with the same bored air as when she delivered the menus.

Both young men ordered a mountain of food, and Annabelle chose pancakes and fruit. Soon, they were all digging into their food, and silence reigned except for the occasional ding of the bell on the door and the chatter of other patrons.

Liev was right about the coffee, though. This is amazing. Annabelle took another sip.

"So." Annabelle lifted bleary eyes to the two men. "You seemed like you were on a mission this morning. What's up?"

Liev and Adler gave each other the side-eye and then Adler spoke up. "Have you read the letters yet?"

"No." She dropped her eyes back to her mostly empty plate and moved the syrup around with her fork. She made a conscious effort to keep her eyes away from her backpack, where the letters were stashed, and away from Adler and Liev, who she could feel staring her down.

"Annabelle," Adler said, his voice even deeper than normal, "You should read them."

"Why?"

Liev jumped in, "Correct me if I'm wrong; you're looking for something, or you're trying to do something, and you're struggling with it?"

"Brilliant deduction. Isn't everyone struggling?" Sarcasm dripped off her words. Annabelle spun in the booth, leaned back against her backpack, and lifted her legs up on the bench, her feet dangling off the edge. "So now that we've established what I will not be doing, was there anything else? Or can I get on with my day?"

From across the table, Adler sighed. "You can get on with your day."

"Thanks for breakfast, fellas." She flashed a peace sign at them as she stood and walked out the front door. The ding of the bell grated on her nerves and her headache. Before she had taken two steps, the bell was ringing again. Liev and Adler were right behind her. She turned left—away from the Keeper's court, and they followed right in step. Annabelle ignored them and continued on toward the river, making as many turns along the way as she could. When it became obvious they weren't going to leave her alone, she turned on them.

"Liev. Adler. You cannot follow me to where I'm going. You just can't. If you've seen there with me, it's not going to go well."

Adler and Liev looked at each other with bewildered faces. Adler grinned at her, "Who's following you? We're just taking a walk!"

"Ugh! I know you're following me. And you can't!" Annabelle grew visibly agitated at the thought of Pedro seeing her with the two agents and misunderstanding. She spun on one heel and stormed off, but the two agents kept in step with her. The more agitated she grew, the more they smiled.

You can't bring them to your spot at the river. That much is crystal clear to you, so you change course. You backtrack toward the garden, leading them away from Pedro and the river and the stashed uniform you had created to mimic theirs. When you reach the garden, you can't help but notice the satisfied grins on the faces of both the young agents.

Liev looked around and said, "Hey, what a great spot! Are we going to go hide in the bushes again?"

Annabelle rolled her eyes at him and headed to her spot on the low wall. The agents followed. She sat down on her low wall and leaned back against the tree, determined to ignore the agents until they grew bored and went away or fell asleep. Liev sat down on the ground, leaning against the tree to her right.

Adler stood next to him, resting one shoulder against it. Across the garden a gangly teen walked in. Annabelle might have missed him completely, but she felt both agents watching him. He traipsed across the garden, arms flailing, looking like he had no idea how long his arms and legs were. He was easily as tall as the agents, but had the peach fuzz of a boy in his early teens. His hair was stick straight, the color of a field of wheat, and it fluttered in the breeze. Annabelle guessed he was probably 15 or so. He headed straight for the gate to the Writer's room and lifted his hand. Annabelle watched him enter, wondering why she felt she had seen him before. It wasn't the usual feeling of deja vu that came from knowing what was in the future book. It was more like he reminded her of someone else, someone she already knew.

You settle into your spot on the low wall and lean back against the tree. The agents follow you but you are careful to ignore them. You'll bore them to death, and they'll either give up and leave, or they'll fall asleep in the quiet of the garden. The Comforter settles to your right on the ground, and The Watcher stands next to him, propped up against the trunk. He begins to whistle a slow, haunting melody that weaves its way around the garden and floats with the breeze through the branches. The melody takes flight with a small blue bird and soars on the wind before coming back to settle in the grass next to you. You're captivated by the song. It wraps itself around you like a warm blanket on a cool day.

When Adler began his whistled tune, Annabelle fought the feeling of coming home. The song filled the garden with its soulful phrasing, and she recognized the tune as the same one that Caretaker would hum as she went through her day. The rich song meandered into its ending, and Annabelle's thoughts wandered back to the teen in the Writer's room.

"Adler? Liev? Can I ask you something?" Her voice sounded unsure to her own ears.

"Sure," Adler responded.

"What do you know about the Future Books?" She rushed ahead, trying to make them understand what she was looking for. "Like, obviously, they tell the future and all that. But have they ever been *wrong* about something? Or can things happen to change it?"

Liev spoke up from his slouched position on the ground. "We actually don't know much about them at all. Like I said, yours is the first I've ever looked into. Why do you ask?" She looked at him and saw he had pulled his hat over his eyes. *I should've kept quiet. He's on his way to sleep!*

"Umm… well, it's just that I don't remember that teenager coming through on this day. And it's more than that. There have been a lot of things lately that don't feel right. Like… what I'm wearing? My Future book said I would be wearing joggers today but I grabbed jeans!"

Adler's voice came from above her head, "When was the last time you opened your book? Maybe you just aren't remembering it, right?"

"I suppose that's possible." Annabelle's brow furrowed and she was shaking her head. "It's been a lot of years… it's just that up until like a week ago, everything happened exactly like I remember it happening."

"Hold on a sec," Liev sat up and pulled his hat back. "What teenager? Are you talking about Isaac?"

"How would I know his name?" Annabelle felt the irritation overtaking the confusion and curiosity.

Adler nodded thoughtfully. "Isaac is our little brother. He's in training to become an agent for the Keeper. Liev thinks he's in line to take on the seal of the ox. I wonder why your future book omitted him today. That's really strange. But when I run into things I can't explain, I turn to the Keeper. He knows it all, and he doesn't mind sharing a lot of it with us. He has the Writer send messages to help us through. You could... read the messages. You've fallen quite behind on what he wants to say to you, and I don't think he's going to send the messenger out again until you've read what he already sent."

The mention of the unopened envelopes in her backpack snapped something inside of Annabelle, and she forgot all about the little agent-in-training. "Listen, I've had enough. I'm leaving, and you're staying here. Or going somewhere else. But what you're not doing is following me, got it? I am not interested in anything the Messenger sends; I don't care *who* it comes from, Writer or Keeper!" She stood and hastily threw her backpack on her back. Checking to make sure the Watcher and Comforter hadn't moved, she turned and stormed out of the garden entry. She didn't slow down all the way through the market, where she grabbed two bottles from a vendor who wasn't looking. She still didn't slow until she threw herself into her chair down by the river. Then she pulled out the first bottle and took a big gulp. It burned on the way down, searing her throat and dulling her agitation.

She was three-quarters of the way through the first bottle when Pedro showed up and helped her finish it and the second one. She didn't object when he pulled her under the bridge and began touching her all over. Instead, she lost herself in the sensations rushing through her body. When they came together like this, she forgot all about his piercing anger and dominating attitude. She just used him to fill the void and distract her for a while. All too soon, it was over, and the emptiness returned. She left Pedro sleeping under the bridge and stumbled her way back to her box before she passed out.

CHAPTER 13

Chapter 6—Day 10
The sunlight feels like it's stabbing through your
eyeballs to the back of your head. Even closing your eyes
does nothing to dull the pain. You roll over to hide from
the light and breathe a sigh of relief as the darkness
takes over again. Next thing you know, someone is
banging on the side of your box and yelling.

"Hey! You know the rules. No daytime loitering in these parts. C'mon, get up and out of there!"

Annabelle groaned. She must have slept late. "Listen," She hollered out to the workers, and then held one hand up to her head to stop the swirling. "I'm coming. I'm just sick is all. Give me a minute."

"You'd better be gone by the time I'm back." The man grunted and he and his friends headed down the alley checking for other violators of the daytime law.

Annabelle knew they were serious, and she also knew she didn't want to end up in lock-up. She had been there a couple of times before. It wasn't pleasant. She looked around her box for her backpack. Panic set in when she realized it wasn't there. *Where did I leave it?* She threw her hair into a messy bun and left her box in the same clothes she had worn the day before. She had to find her backpack. Her Future Book was in it! She would love to get rid of the Future Book altogether, but she couldn't have it falling into the wrong hands. Thinking through the night before, she was pretty sure she had left it at the river. Her story was not safe in Pedro's hands, especially the ending! Thinking about him reading her book pushed her to a jog and then a full-out run.

The river came into view and she could see there was no one in her chair. She breathed a sigh of relief until she saw the ground around it. Scattered everywhere were the messages from the Writer. Some were crumpled, some were torn into pieces. She started gathering the pieces, looking as she went for her backpack and Future Book. The trail of black paper and envelopes led down to the water, where she found some soaked and damaged beyond recognition. There, lodged into some rocks, was her backpack. She grabbed it hastily and opened it. Her Future Book was still inside. She quickly gathered the rest of the messages, shivering at the thought of Pedro reading through them. Pedro was nowhere in sight, but she didn't know how long he had with her book before she got there. He might have had time to get into the Future Book. He would know how the story ends. He would *know* that she had no intention of allowing him to profit from the plan to steal artwork from the other side of the island. If that was the case, she would be dead before she had a chance to change the ending.

Annabelle crumpled into her seat and tried to think through the pages of the Future Book to the next time she would see Pedro. But she could only get two things into focus. The current moment and the end. She closed her eyes. Her head was swimming, making it hard to think at all.

You close your eyes, trying to picture the pages of the

Future Book, but the pages grow hazy. You're certain that it's a result of the wicked hangover pounding through your head. With a frustrated sigh, you give up. You throw your head back against the chair and become still. You feel the sun on your face and hear the trickle of water flowing around the rocks in the river. The pressure in your head eases ever so slightly. You realize the fist full of messages is still in your left hand, and your open backpack with the Future Book inside is in your right. You transfer the messages to the backpack and drop it on the ground without ever opening your eyes or lifting your head. You're hungry, but the pull of being still and quiet overpowers the pull of your empty stomach, so you remain in place. You feel like you could stay like this all day, but it's not too long before you hear a whistle split the quiet. The piercing noise bounces around your head like a pinball, setting off sparks of pain everywhere it hits. You open your eyes and watch Pedro approach. If the evil glint in his eye is any indication, he has read plenty.

"Well, well. What do we have here? Looks like a lying, cheating, scheming, worthless ____." His final word was less than complimentary. Pedro interlaced his fingers and stretched out his arms, cracking every knuckle. Anxiety clawed up Annabelle's throat, but she swallowed it down and stared directly into his eyes.

"*Me*, cheating. Ha!" She retorted, "I know where you've been and every woman that you've screwed. Don't even get started on me." She flipped him off and turned her head away from him. She knew it was a play to get him off her back and one she could scarcely afford to make. Unfortunately, he knew it, too. He grabbed her arm with one hand and forced her chin back toward him with the other.

"I know *everything* about you now, you filth." He got in her face. She tried to pull away, but his grip was too tight. "I know every lie. Every scheme. I own you." Only then did he release her with a jerk. He stood over her. Terror filled her heart. He knew everything and she had lost the game. "It's a shame those messages got destroyed by the water. From what I read, they were vital to your survival." He turned and walked away, up toward the road, throwing a parting shot over his shoulder. "And if you want to know what they say, you're gonna have to do what *I* say." The echo of his cruel laughter floated back toward her even after he turned the corner.

Annabelle sat in her chair, stupefied. Scenes from her past swirled through her head. One-night stands, drunken liaisons. The times she had taken more than her share of the take. The lies she told him to keep him satisfied. One after another, they paraded past, and after each one, she groaned at the thought of Pedro reading all about them.

You sit in your chair, cursing yourself, cursing Pedro, cursing the Writer and the Keeper and the Messenger. Thinking of the Messenger sends your thoughts to the messages that Pedro read. Understanding what Pedro had said creeps into your mind slowly; your survival depends on the messages you never read. The same messages that Pedro read and deliberately destroyed. Filled with a sudden need to know what it was the messages say, you think maybe you'll be able to recover the soaked notes and you scramble to the water. When you pull the soaked papers out of the water and smooth them on your knee, you see that the writing on them isn't legible. It isn't even there. It's like the water completely washed the writing away. You imagine Pedro's smug laugh as he crumpled each message and threw it in the water.

The sound of laughter grew in Annabelle's mind until she noticed that it wasn't in her imagination after all; Pedro was back. Annabelle stood, allowing the washed-out messages to fall to the ground, and turned toward where Pedro stood. His face was cold as ice, and hers matched it. She stared at him silently, waiting for whatever torment his evil mind had concocted in the few moments since he walked away.

After what seemed like forever, he broke the silence: "You know, it really doesn't help me any to have all this power over you if you're not with me. So. Let's go. You're coming with me."

"You've forgotten something," Annabelle retorted. "I don't *want* to know what was in those messages. That's why I didn't open them in the first place."

Pedro laughed a cold, cruel laugh and pointed at the wet spot on the knee of her pants. "So you're telling me that you didn't just try to pull them out of the river and read them? Please. I'm not buying what you're selling. Let's... go." The last words were delivered with deadly calm.

Annabelle deflated. She scrambled for another play but couldn't come up with anything, and her mind was too scattered to think through the coming pages of the Future Book. So she shouldered her bag and moved up the slope to the road where Pedro stood, grinning now that he was assured of her total compliance. As they started walking, he started talking.

"I thought we'd start out with a simple robbery. There's a shop near here that's run by this wicked hot girl. I've been hitting on her for weeks, and she keeps shutting me down, and I'm getting sick of it." Pedro was watching her carefully and apparently satisfied by her disgust. He nodded. "So what better way to get back at her than to have *you* empty the cash register while I distract her." He grinned at Annabelle. "I should warn you, though, they do have a security guard."

Out loud Annabelle just answered, "Great." In her head was a whole different story. *How am I going to figure out what was in the messages? Pedro will never let go of the power over me and it doesn't seem like he'll leave me alone to find another way, either.* She contemplated asking the Writer to give her a new set of messages, but feared angering him. Liev and Adler *might* help, but only with the ok from the Messenger.

Annabelle's frantic thoughts covered up whatever else Pedro had been saying. She had been walking behind him and almost barreled right into him when he abruptly stopped in front of a shop advertising a sale on "medicinal" herbs. Through the window, Annabelle spotted a sweet young girl standing at the cash register. She had pretty, flowing brown hair, blue eyes, and perfect pale skin. It was like looking through a window to her past. Annabelle looked over at Pedro and saw through his innocent look to the devil behind his eyes. He was telling her he was done with her. He was looking for a newer, younger model. Bitterness wrapped its way around her heart, at one point, that would've hurt. Now, it was just another reminder that her time was running out. Annabelle breathed in deeply, bracing herself for the moments ahead. Not that she cared about the girl or the stealing. Not at all. But she couldn't risk getting caught today, and she didn't have any time to prepare herself.

Pedro had already walked in and sauntered up to the counter. The girl was clearly annoyed. Her body language suggested she was protecting herself from him. She angled her body away from him, keeping her shoulder lifted. Annabelle pushed the door open. Making it look like she was browsing through the merchandise, she worked her way through the room, ending near the cash register. Pedro was pushing hard for the girl to go out with him. The girl was working hard to maintain a polite but distant smile. Annabelle felt almost bad for her.

She cut into the conversation, "Hey, excuse me. I could use some help. Could you tell this loser 'no' after you help me?" Annabelle jerked her thumb in Pedro's direction. The girl's relief was palpable.

"Oh, certainly!" The girl's relief was obvious as she turned to Pedro and said, "Will you please excuse me for a moment?" Without waiting for a response, she gave her full attention to Annabelle. "What can I help you with?"

Annabelle led her away from the register to the far corner of the store. "I'm having trouble with my knee. It hurts when I keep it in one position for too long. Which one of these would you recommend?" She held out two types of cream to the girl. Across the store, Pedro was messing with some of the other products, noisily moving them to where they didn't belong. Annabelle figured he would work with her plan—they had pulled a similar one-off before—but since he didn't give her a chance to talk it out beforehand, she was still nervous. The security guard in the back of the store didn't help her butterflies at all.

The girl was holding out one of the creams to her. Annabelle smiled, took it, and said, "Thanks." As they moved back to the register, Annabelle tried to subtly signal Pedro to distract the girl once the register drawer was open. The girl rang up the order and gave her the total. Annabelle pulled some change out of her bag and started counting it out into the girl's hand. She hit a button on the register, and the drawer slid open. Just as she started counting the coins and depositing them into the drawer, Pedro grabbed her by the wrist.

"Hey! What are you doing!?! Let me go!" The girl yelled, drawing the security guard's attention. Pedro was fast, however. He hauled her over near the door and pushed her against a display case with his body. The security guard was fast, too, and as he tackled Pedro, Annabelle emptied the drawer into her backpack. She was finished in no time, and she moved quickly to the door. She bolted out and down the road back toward the river by a circuitous route with frequent backward glances to be sure she wasn't being followed. On her way, she dug out about a hundred from the bag and tucked it inside her bra. After a moment, she thought better of it and moved half of it to her shoe. There was no telling what kind of mood Pedro would be in after that display, and she couldn't take any chances.

You breathe a sigh of relief as you reach the water.

Your chair beckons you to let down your guard for just a moment. The day had been crazy from the beginning. Pausing allows you a chance to notice your empty stomach. You haven't even eaten yet today.

"How much did we get?" Pedro's voice shattered her moment of peace.

She languidly held out her backpack to him. "Beats me. Count it yourself." He grabbed the bag and pulled out the cash. He dug around in the bag until he was satisfied that he had gotten every dollar, then tossed the bag back to her. He gleefully counted it, then turned his attention back to Annabelle.

"So where's the rest?" he asked demandingly.

"The rest of what?" Annabelle tipped her head down and looked up at Pedro sardonically.

"The rest of the cash. Where did you stash it?" He walked over and stared down at her. Then he leaned over and tugged on the neck of her shirt. "Your bra, right?" He stopped. "No, wait. It wouldn't be there. Your shoes." She didn't move as he pulled off her left shoe first and then her right. When he pulled off the right shoe, several bills fluttered to the ground. Pedro slapped Annabelle across the face and picked up the bills. He shook them in her face before he walked back to the pile of cash, shoving all of it into his pockets and making his way up the bank.

At the top, he turned his head and said, "Mess with me again, and I'll kill you," before he walked out of sight. Annabelle leaned over the arm of her chair and dry heaved, releasing all the stress of the morning. When she again opened her eyes with her head still hanging low, she noticed a black envelope just in front of her chair. She snatched it up. This couldn't be one of the messages from earlier; they were all either in her bag or by the water. Besides, this one was still in its envelope. Annabelle frantically opened it, hoping against hope it would be a new copy of the vital messages that had been destroyed. It registered in her mind as she read it that the writing was once again the kind of shimmery print, but she shrugged off the nagging sense that something wasn't right. This could give her a clue to how to survive past the last page of her book. She focused on the message:

Pedro didn't read the whole book. Now is your chance to take control.

The message slowly crumpled as Annabelle closed her fist around it. *The Liar! No wonder he wouldn't let me read the messages.* She made a silent vow to make him pay for the lies and for taunting her with the younger girl. A shadow skittered over the sun, making Annabelle shiver. A dark thought grew in her mind, and a plan began to take shape. She *would* turn the tables on Pedro. She walked to the river and dropped the message in it. Then she pivoted and walked away without noticing that when the water washed over the writing, the letters lost their shine and turned blood red.

CHAPTER 14

Chapter 6—Day 10, afternoon

Your mind clears as you walk. The writing of the Future Book grows clear and dark in your head, and you're pretty sure this plan will work. In fact, it will utterly devastate Pedro. It's a sucker punch to his gut. You laugh to yourself just thinking about it. You look down at the white mark on your right hand and the empty palm of your left. It won't stay empty for long, but sticking it to Pedro is totally worth it. Thinking ahead through the Future Book shows you exactly when to strike —not until the day you take The Comforter's place on the truck. That means you've got three days of avoiding Pedro. It shouldn't be too hard. Pedro never goes near the Keeper's Court or the Garden. You can camp out in the bushes for three days, but first, you'll need some supplies. On your way to the Garden, you stop at a corner store.

Before you walk in, you pull out a couple of bills from your bra. You make short work of choosing a few foods that will stay good for a couple of days. When you get to the checkout, you confuse the cashier and trade bills with her just enough that you walk away with twenty more than you brought in with you.

*A*nnabelle couldn't help but smirk as she walked out of the store, stuffing the cash back inside her bra. She wandered slowly toward the Garden. Pedro had pockets full of cash; he would be on his way to the north shore, where there were plenty of places dedicated to almost legal ways to spend it. Once she got to the Garden, she settled into her hidden nest behind the bushes. She pulled out some food and tried to eat, but the drowsiness took over, and she drifted off to sleep and into the same dream that had been haunting her.

Conrad's back is turned toward her. She begs and pleads, pulling on her little brother's arms and his shirt, trying everything she can think of to move him, but he's as immovable as a statue. His face doesn't change expression, he just stares straight ahead at the gate, arms crossed and feet spread apart. No matter what she tries, Annabelle cannot get past him. Sobbing, she turns back toward the path through the woods. Conrad said she had to walk through the path to get to the other side, and it seemed there was no other option open to her. So she headed down the path once more, passing Caretaker and then Protector. She didn't look up at them. She couldn't bear seeing the tears on their faces even one more time. When she came close to Rosa, she started to jog, wanting to get past her as quickly as possible. She saw the machete and bag and then the smoldering money on the ground where she had dropped it.

She grabbed the machete and started swinging, but she couldn't seem to make any progress. Suddenly, the undergrowth felt more like metal, and the machete didn't make a dent in it. She swung furiously for a few moments, then stopped, panting. She dropped the machete point down to the ground where it stuck and tried to think what to do. Looking back, she knew that when she was carrying the bag from Caretaker, the machete worked just fine. She picked up the bag and then yanked the machete out of the ground. Going back to the brush, she started swinging again. This time, the vines and sprouting trees felt more like rubber; they bounced back after every swing. Annabelle let out a yell, "What do you expect me to do?!?"

A whisper on the wind answered her, "Pick up the money."

Annabelle skulked back to where the money lay and picked it up with her left hand. She immediately felt a burning sensation. Dropping the money she saw the mark on her right hand now matched the one on her left. Both marks were black as night. Seeing no way around it, she picked up the money again and went back to clearing the path. This time, it worked like it should. She pressed on through the woods, feeling as if she would never find the other side. The dense growth slowly gave way to a lighter path.

Annabelle almost stumbled over the next person—a tall, thin teen with brown flowing hair. It took Annabelle a moment to place her; then she connected her with the robbery earlier in the day. The girl was laying near the path, curled up in a ball. Her clothes were covered with mud. The whisper in the breeze told her to trade sweatshirts with the muddy girl. She started putting down the things she was holding so she could take the sweatshirt off.

You wake up with a groan. You want to shake the dream off of you, but it hangs in the air like an oppressive humidity, making it hard to breathe. You start to get the sense there's a reason you woke up, so you work to open your eyes. Your eyelids feel heavy and your limbs are wooden as you try to move. You end up sitting before your eyes are fully opened. When you do open them, there isn't anything obvious that stands out as something that would have woken you. You stand up and stretch, trying to clear your mind and regain control of your muscles.

Annabelle sat up, eyes still mostly closed. When she opened them, she immediately saw the young man from earlier—the one the agents had called Isaac. He was standing near her nest but facing away from her. When he heard her moving, he turned with a huge smile on his face.

"Hey there! You're up!"

Annabelle tried to answer but ended up making a noise more like a cross between a cough and a moan. She cleared her throat and tried again. "Uh, hey. Isaac, right?"

"Yeah!" His smile grew even wider. "How did you know?"

"Your brothers told me."

"Aw, that's cool! You know Liev and Adler?" His bright blue eyes were filled with happiness at the mention of his brothers. "They are the coolest ever. They've been agents for the Keeper for a couple of years now, and I can't wait to finish my training period so I can be one too!" He looked up at the statue of the ox with awe in his face. "Can you even imagine being an agent for the Keeper?!?"

Annabelle didn't know what it was about this kid, but he stirred something different in her. She wanted to give him a snarky reply, but the look on his face was so hopeful and innocent that she just couldn't. "Yeah, kid, that's gonna be really cool." She smiled back at him.

"I think the Keeper is amazing. Think of how he keeps everything running around here and protects us. He created this *whole island* and cares about everyone on it. He takes care of all those kids who don't have parents or whose parents can't take care of them. He gives everyone a purpose and helps them make it happen. And he still has time to send *everyone* messages whenever they need them! And…"

Annabelle got the impression he could have gone on for days. Instead, she interrupted his flow of thought, "Is he really all that great that you'd want to spend your whole life doing what he says? Don't you have dreams of your own?"

Isaac shook his head. His hair flopped back and forth, adding emphasis to the fierce shake of his head. "For as long as I can remember, all I've ever wanted to do is serve the Keeper. He's done such great things, so why wouldn't I want to serve him? Also, I want to be just like my brothers. They do important work." He paused, then tipped his head as though deep in thought, "How do *you* know Liev and Adler?"

"Me? Oh, well..." The question made Annabelle wonder how she *knew* the two agents. "Um, I guess we just kinda met one day. I was in the garden, and Adler started talking to me. Then Liev showed up. Actually, they've kinda made themselves pests, hanging around all the time and interrupting my plans." Isaac's brow furrowed, so Annabelle laughed to show him she wasn't upset. "You're right, though, they're really great guys. I can see why you'd want to be like them."

"You mean, *both* Adler and Liev have been hanging around you for more than like a day?" Isaac studied her face intently. "You must be someone really important!" His smile shone like the sun, and his eyes were as dazzling as the sky around it. Annabelle almost believed him for half a second. Then reality crashed in.

"Me? No. I'm not important at all." The flash of hope made the crash back to reality even harder to stomach than normal. "I'm no one. I never have been. And my Future Book says I never will be."

"Hmm. That can't be right. Liev and Adler are currently the *only* two agents of the Keeper on the West side. He wouldn't waste their time like that if it didn't matter." His confusion didn't hold back his optimism for long. His sunny outlook took over quickly. "You must be missing something! Have you asked the Keeper?"

"Have I...? No, I haven't, I mean..." Annabelle didn't want to dampen the kid's enthusiasm, but she also had no intention of asking the Keeper for anything. She smiled gently at him, "I love the way you think, Isaac. Thanks for the idea."

"I know! Let's go talk to the Writer!" He grabbed her wrist and practically cantered across the garden, dragging her along behind him to the gate.

"Wait, Isaac, hold on!" Annabelle gasped and panted, trying to keep up and pull free at the same time.

"C'mon, Annabelle, Let's go in!" His eyes pleaded with hers, but something nagged at her mind.

"Wait a minute, how do you know my name?" She stopped herself from yanking her arm back. This kid was too sweet, and his uncomplicated belief in the goodness of the Keeper radiated from him. She couldn't destroy him the way she had so many others.

Isaac laughed. It was a full-bellied, joy-filled, child-like laugh with no malice whatsoever in it. "Oh, yes! I suppose I should have told you when we first met! You'll have to forgive me; this is my very first mission on my own. I'm not great at it yet."

"Mission?" She took a step back. She didn't like the idea of being anyone's mission.

"Yeah!" He stepped forward to be closer to her. "Well, actually, my mission is to bring you into the Writer's room with me, but I forgot all about it because I got so excited to bring you in! The Writer's Room is my *favorite* place in the whole world. There isn't a better place *anywhere*! And I really want to share it with you, will you come with me? Please?" He smiled his sweet, pure smile. It felt funny to be looking up at someone so young. More than anything, Annabelle wanted to say, "No," but his blue eyes pleaded with her and tore apart all her defenses. She could hardly be the one to make him fail his first assignment. She agreed with a simple nod and was rewarded with a smile that could power a small city. The tears at the corner of his eyes told Annabelle beyond the shadow of a doubt that he was telling her the truth—it was more about sharing this with her than it was about fulfilling a mission. Her heart lifted and the feeling carried her through the gate and down the stairs through the door into the Writer's room.

But when she stepped inside, confusion ripped through her. If Isaac had loosened his grip on her wrist, she would have felt as though she had stepped into another dimension, but the firm pressure kept her grounded. The room was nothing like what it had been before. The attic room had disappeared, and with it, the couch, chair, and rocker. There was no place for drawing or writing and no railing or stairs. In fact, there were no walls at all. Annabelle found herself standing barefoot on tightly packed sand, listening to the rhythm of waves crashing on the shore. She tipped her head back and saw thousands of stars in clusters and waves across a midnight blue sky. Even without the moon, she could see across the beach, the waves in the water, and the hills behind the beach. A little way down the beach, she saw a fire and a man hunkered down next to it.

After soaking in the scene in front of her, Annabelle looked back to Isaac's glowing face. His smile stretched across his face, and he was bouncing with excitement. He tugged on her arm, hollering, "Come on, let's go!" He then released her and ran with arms flailing toward the man and the fire as fast as his gangly legs would take him. Annabelle couldn't resist the excitement radiating from his person and she took off after him with a laugh and a "Wait up!" By the time they got to the fire, neither one of them could breathe. They collapsed on the sand in a fit of playful giggles.

Annabelle laughed until she cried. The tears that fell down her cheeks and soaked into the sand felt as if they were drawing out all her anger, pain, and brokenness. Her bitterness seemed to fade away like the drops sinking out of sight. She felt a hand gently resting on her forehead and occasionally stroking her hair, which had fallen out of its holder and was now splayed wildly around her head. Thinking it had to be sweet Isaac, she allowed the defenses around her heart to crack open, just a little, and be touched by the tender gesture. The ache in the back of her head subsided, and she released the tension that had been holding each muscle hostage for days, or perhaps even longer. She felt like a child as the tears cascaded down her face.

"I *knew* you would love it here!" Isaac's voice floated over to her from closer to the fire. "Writer! Do you see those tears? Wait, of course you do!" Isaac laughed at his own silly question.

"Yes, dear Isaac, I see." The Writer laughed with him from above Annabelle's head. Her eyes slammed open, and she looked up into the dancing eyes of the Writer. Before she could formulate any words, the Writer winked at her and stood. He held his hand down to her to lift her to standing as well while saying, "You must be hungry, little one. Come and have some fish with us! I see Isaac couldn't wait." And he laughed again as Isaac juggled a scalding hot fish from one hand to another, all while taking small bites of it.

"Mmmph." Isaac said between bites, "This... is really... really good.... You should try some!" And Annabelle couldn't help but laugh again as she sat down next to the fire and grabbed another fish on a wooden skewer from the flames. The heavenly smell overpowered her good sense, and she, too, began devouring the perfectly cooked but ridiculously hot fish.

The Writer laughed again, and the deep, rich sound went ringing out over the waves. "I made plenty; you can take your time, you two! Ha! You would think this boy has never eaten before, the way he scarfs the food down. But he only just left here ten minutes ago to go get you. He's been eating all day!"

Isaac laughed with the Writer, "Well, I can't help it, your fish is so good! And besides, I think I'm growing. Gotta keep up the nutrition, right?"

The Writer smiled at him then. "You are growing, young man. And your greatest test is still ahead of you. So, eat up. As long as you keep coming here, I will keep giving you everything you need." Annabelle looked up from her food long enough to see the Writer wipe one tear off his cheek, then gave the fish her full attention again. The uncomfortable feeling that she was intruding in a private moment washed over her and then passed by, leaving her feeling intimately cherished by both the Writer and the hungry little agent-in-training.

Once the drive of hunger settled down, Annabelle ate more slowly, savoring every bite of the perfectly seasoned fish. She sat watching the flames and the waves and joining in the laughter frequently shared by the Writer and his agent. She had never felt such tenderness before. Even the evident care between the Writer and Annabelle's Caretaker paled in comparison to the deep affection that passed between these two. On the part of the Writer, there was a sadness mixed in with laughter and joy, but the young agent-to-be simply and freely basked in Writer's love. If they hadn't both been so free with their tenderness and care, she would feel dreadfully out of place here, but their kindness drew her in. She forgot all about Future Books and evil boyfriends and fear. Wave after wave of peace washed over her, mimicking the rolling of the water. When it came time to leave, Annabelle followed Isaac's lead and took a flying leap into the Writer's arms. When he wrapped his arms around her, she flashed back to a time when her Protector had thought she was sleeping and picked her up to carry her to her room. It was the same feeling of utter security and love. When she pulled back and the Writer let go, she stammered out a thank you, blushed, and followed Isaac back to the door.

The world outside had gone from afternoon to night in the time that they were gone. Annabelle couldn't believe how much time had passed. She grabbed Isaac in a bear hug before he walked away, and she floated back to her nest in the bushes. She sighed as she laid down on the soft grass and drifted off to sleep. For the first time in weeks, she slept without dreaming.

CHAPTER 15

Chapter 6—Day 11

The sunlight filters through the trees and flutters over your eyes. You were in such a deep, restful sleep that it takes a moment for you to understand where you are. The first thing you remember is the wide open beaches inside the Writer's room. You hardly recognize the you that took a flying leap into the Writer's arms, the you that laughed and ran and played. Yesterday feels like a dream of happiness that can't truly be yours. Reality barges in, shredding the thin veil of peace and belonging that encompassed you when you were with the Writer. Pedro's face imposes itself over the idyllic frames of joy, forcing you to grapple with the cold truth. Betrayal, deception, and murder are your real life.

*A*nnabelle tried to hold onto the peace of the night before. She had never felt so at home as she did on that beach. The campfire smell clung to her, tantalizing her with memories of simple joy. While she was in the Writer's Room with Isaac, the rest of the world had faded away; there was no Pedro, no knife, no Future Book threatening her life. She closed her eyes and pictured the Writer's laughing face. The crinkled corners of his eyes framed kind brown eyes that seemed to look into the deepest parts of her but without disappointment, anger, or fear. Annabelle didn't have a word for what she saw there. She just knew it felt almost like when Protector and Caretaker looked at her sometimes. But there was always something extra in their eyes that made her squirm. That thing wasn't in the Writer's eyes. His eyes were pure. She wanted to believe the message she found there, but as she lost herself in the feelings of the night before, the final words written in her Future Book were superimposed over the image:

You drop your bloodied knife moments before you black out and land on it. You will not wake up the next day.

The peace disintegrated. The anger returned. *How could he look at me like that, even though he wrote what he did?!?* Looking into his eyes, she would *never* have been able to tell that he so callously wrote murder into the end of her story. The contrast between the kindness she felt from him and the words he wrote in her book stirred up a whirlwind in her soul. And then the whirlwind grew and became more turbulent. The feeling created a growing pressure within her. She only knew one or two ways to release all the pressure. Her first thought was Pedro and a steamy session under the bridge, but she was trying to avoid him for a couple of days. Without that option, she decided to go steal some breakfast instead.

You jump up, unwilling to deal with the emotions inside any longer, and start a furious walk toward the market. Anger, fear, and sadness, you aren't willing to acknowledge all vie for the top position, so you quickly promote anger above the others. You've been wronged. Betrayed. Allowing the Writer to breach your walls for even a moment was foolish. You can't seem to recall why you did or even how you got into the Writer's room in the first place.

It was Isaac. The thought stopped Annabelle in her tracks. She went back over the last line in her Future Book inside her mind.

You can't seem to recall why you did or even how you got into the Writer's room in the first place.

But she knew exactly how she got into the Writer's Room! She frantically flipped back the pages in her mind to the day before. The image was blurred, and she couldn't get it to clear up, but she was certain there had been no mention of Isaac. It was like he didn't exist. Panic rose in her chest. She thought back to the day she first saw Isaac and remembered that the book hadn't mentioned him that day either. Page after page of words in the Future Book that didn't add up with the actual events flashed in front of her face in quick succession. With each new picture, her anxiety level escalated until she felt as if she couldn't breathe. She felt exposed and weak out on the street, so she broke into a run toward the nearest alley she could find. Once she was secured and out of sight, she fell onto her knees. The ground had loose gravel on it that ripped through her pants and scraped her knee, but Annabelle didn't care. Actually, it helped. The pain helped her regain some control over her breathing and heartbeat. She pressed her knee into the gravel and gulped in the air. *What happens next?*

You can't seem to recall why you did or even how you got into the Writer's Room in the first place. Instead of speculating further, you decide to harness the anger. You resolve never to allow the Writer that close to you ever again. You get up on your feet and continue toward the market.

Annabelle wiped away an angry tear that had slipped down her cheek. *Harness your anger. Get on your feet.* She stood and brushed her hands down the front of her pants, dislodging the debris that clung to them. If only she could brush off the swirling uncertainty as easily. Her hand clenched into a fist. She wished she had fingernails long enough to dig into her palm. Instead, she bit the inside of her lip, and all of her scattered, spinning thoughts slowly honed in on the pain. The murkiness in her head settled and she chose the easier way—she chose the anger. With her head now clear, she set off toward the market. Today, she would not settle for anything less than what she wanted. As she walked, the words of the Future Book intruded.

You peruse the market with an eye for the priciest pastries and rarest fruits you can find. After looking through most of the market and finding only standard breakfast foods, you settle on a light and flaky pastry filled with cream and jam. You also find a perfectly ripe mango. You're about to head back to the river when you remember that you are avoiding Pedro. You reluctantly make your way back to the garden with your food.

Annabelle got to the market and looked around. She couldn't see why she would bother to walk through it all when she knew already what she would walk away with. At the second booth, she spotted a pastry that fit the description in the Future Book. She quickly assessed the situation. The owner was busy negotiating with an older woman. He seemed to be losing ground to her. A couple of other customers waited with various breads in hand. No one was paying attention to her. She reached out her hand to swipe the pastry and was shocked when another hand reached for the same one. She jerked her hand back and looked up into the dancing blue eyes of Isaac.

"Annabelle!" His grin stretched from ear to ear. "Hey, did you want this one? I can grab something else. It just looked so good. Listen, let me get it for you. I'll have…" He looked over the booth excitedly, "this one!" He held up another kind of pastry. It looked almost like a flower with a million paper-thin petals. He held up a cloth bag. "I already got a bunch of fruit and some sort of egg casserole. We can have a breakfast feast together!"

His enthusiasm and cheer disarmed her in an instant. Her anger dissolved. She bit down on the inside of her cheek, but even the sharp pain couldn't conjure the rage of just moments before. If it had been anyone else, she could have spat out something sarcastic and angry and walked away. But something about Isaac left her defenseless. He was too innocent to have a hidden motive. The only thing he wanted from her was breakfast—a picnic together. No agenda. No angle. So, instead of lashing out at him, she smiled.

"Look at what I've got!" Isaac exclaimed excitedly, holding the bag open for her to see.

Annabelle's eyes widened at the riches he carried. "Where did you find grapes? I haven't seen any in ages! They don't grow in Canree Nu!"

"Oh! The writer told me they're your favorite, and I asked a friend of mine who travels to the mainland pretty regularly if he would bring them for me. He just got in this morning." Isaac flashed his sweet smile at her and turned to the owner to buy the pastries. In the time the conversation took, the negotiations between the booth owner and the older woman had wrapped up, and the owner had made short work of selling to the other customers. It wasn't long at all before

Annabelle and Isaac were headed to the garden with their breakfast feast.

When they arrived, Isaac didn't head for one of the picnic tables like Annabelle expected. Instead, he headed straight for the gate to the Writer's Room. Annabelle stopped a couple of steps short of the entrance. Before she could say anything, Isaac raised his free hand, and Annabelle heard the familiar clank of the gate opening. Isaac pulled the gate open and stood against it to let her through.

Annabelle's feet felt like lead. It was less than an hour ago that she was broiling with anger at the Writer. She didn't want to go into his room again. She didn't want to feel the things she felt in there, only to come back out to reality once again. But there was Isaac, with his smile starting to fade and his sandy blond eyebrows knitting together in concern.

"Annabelle?" Isaac's voice sounded uncertain, and she couldn't bear to be the one to take the smile off his face. She mustered up a smile and pushed herself to move in through the gate. As she brushed past Isaac, he asked her, "Is everything ok?"

"Everything is great! I can't wait to dig into all that amazing fruit!" She smiled at him, but it was forced. She felt hollow. She ducked her head down as she made her way through the door. Once again, her eyes took a moment to adjust to the darkness.

When you make your way through the gate, you're enveloped once again in the night sky. A cool breeze dances around you. The heaviness of the moment before is lifted off your shoulders. Your mind clears, and peaceful joy fills your heart. Lifting the food bag out to the side, you accelerate into a run. Down the beach you see the familiar figure of the Writer next to a glowing flame.

Annabelle rolled her eyes at the Future Book's account. She turned back to Isaac who had just entered the Writer's Room, carrying the food. Shoving reality away, she grabbed his free hand, and together, they ran and laughed and stumbled, struggling back to their feet until they reached the fire. Annabelle laughed at the thought of eating their luscious breakfast feast by a fire on the beach under the stars. Isaac and the Writer clasped hands.

"Isaac, welcome back! And you brought Annabelle again!" The Writer turned to where Annabelle stood, "Hello, Annabelle. I'm delighted to see you." Annabelle couldn't say the same, so she only offered a tight-lipped smile.

Thankfully, Isaac didn't notice. He had already begun unpacking the food and chattering away. When he got to the grapes, he immediately broke off a bunch and bounced over to where Annabelle was sitting, dropping them into her open hands. Annabelle instantly plucked one off the vine and popped it into her mouth. When she bit down, flavor flooded her mouth, and joy flooded her heart.

She didn't wait to swallow; she just lifted a hand in front of her mouth and talked around the grape, "This is the most amazing thing I've ever tasted in my life!"

"I told Isaac grapes are your favorite. I'm so happy he was able to get some for you." The Writer grabbed a stick and stoked the fire.

"Why? Why did you tell him they're my favorite? Why would you want him to get them for me?" Annabelle asked the question around another mouthful of grapes.

"I'd like to think that someday you will choose to come through the gate on your own and not just with your Caretaker or with young Isaac here. Maybe next time you think of grapes… you will think of this space, too, and want to come."

Annabelle doubted it. Instead of responding, she stuffed another grape in her mouth and mumbled something purposely incoherent.

"Wait, you haven't ever come here by yourself?" Incredulous, Isaac blurted out the question like the teenager he was. Annabelle opened her mouth to answer, but then it was as if a lightbulb turned on for Isaac, and he looked to the Writer, "What does her room look like?"

Annabelle's head snapped up. "I have my own room? Like *this*? Like Caretaker does?"

"Yes." The Writer's voice was clear and gentle. When he didn't elaborate after a moment, Isaac and Annabelle both began talking.

"But what does it look like?"

"Let's leave and come back into *your* room! Can we do that?"

The Writer's eyes crinkled up at the corners, exposing his enjoyment of the situation. "I'm not going to tell you, Annabelle. And Isaac, no. You can't."

Annabelle's and Isaac's mouths flew open. Annabelle was tempted to whine at the Writer, but she figured it would do no good. Isaac, seeing that the Writer was serious, harrumphed and crossed his arms playfully.

The Writer smiled and softly asked, "Now, do I get some of that delicious fruit, or is Annabelle going to devour every last grape on her own?"

Both Annabelle and Isaac jumped up and finished pulling the goodies out of the bag. Isaac had thought of everything, including plates and forks. The three of them feasted until their bellies were stuffed. Then they lay on the beach while Isaac and Annabelle speculated on what her room would look like and why. The Writer would throw in impossibly ridiculous options, making the other two laugh and snort. They talked and laughed for hours. Annabelle grew drowsy and fell asleep but didn't realize it until she woke later to Isaac nudging her and asking if she wanted any more grapes. She didn't say anything in response, just held out her hand. Isaac dropped another bunch into it.

"So, really, I have a room. If I opened the gate, I would come into a totally different room." She looked up questioningly at the Writer.

"Truly. You and I have our own space to meet with each other. And you can come in anytime you like." The Writer paused, then continued gently, "I've given you the key to the gate."

Annabelle looked down at the palm of her hand. "Yeah, well, mine's broken." She stood and hurriedly continued, "Hey, Isaac. We've been here all day again, man. It's time to head out." She sniffed and looked at the ground. Isaac looked back and forth between her and the Writer, who also stood.

"Actually, Isaac, if you're able to, I'd love to talk with just you for a little bit. Would that be ok?" The Writer looked to Isaac, and then to Annabelle, eyebrows lifted in question. Isaac nodded right away. It took Annabelle a moment to realize he was actually asking her, too, if it was alright. When she figured it out, she stuttered out, "Oh, uh yeah, sure. Of course." Then she looked to Isaac and said, "I'll catch you later, kid. Thanks for the food."

Discontented with the disconnected farewell, Isaac swept Annabelle up in a giant bear hug, lifting her off her feet. "Today was the best! Weren't those grapes amazing? I could eat grapes every day!"

Annabelle smiled at his enthusiasm and assured him that the grapes were indeed delicious. Grapes every day? She would kill for that. Truthfully, she would give anything to live in this joy every day. To eat grapes and talk by the fire. To soak in the pure, radiant peace, Isaac seemed to carry with him everywhere he went. It was a nice dream, but it was time for her to get back to reality. Isaac had pinned her arms down in the hug, but she wiggled one arm around enough to awkwardly pat his back. He spun her around and unceremoniously deposited her back on the ground.

Once she was back on her own feet, Annabelle gave a small wave to Isaac and the Writer and reluctantly trudged up the sandy hill to the door. Before she stepped out, she took one final look back. The Writer and Isaac were already deep in conversation, heads close together. As she looked, the Writer lifted his hand to the side of Isaac's face. Then the gate clanged shut behind her, and she was alone in the garden. It had been her choice to leave the Writer's Room. Deep inside, she knew that. But the clanging gate echoed around her heart, ringing out an all too familiar song of being on the outside. She was alone. Shut out. And another poisonous drop of bitterness doused the joy.

CHAPTER 16

Chapter 6—Day 12, early in the morning
A loud crash pulls you out of a deep sleep, and the feelings of the night before wash over you like a flood, drowning you in their intensity.

A crack of thunder broke through Annabelle's consciousness, and heavy drops of rain pelted her through her clothing. The flood of rain soon left her gasping as she jumped toward the base of a nearby tree. Lightening split the sky, and she knew she had to find better cover quickly. She had seen storms like this one before. Mentally flipping through her options, Annabelle realized her best bet was Caretaker's house. She groaned out loud. She had last seen Caretaker in the Writer's Room, a smile on her face and a look in her eyes that was filled with hope but also a cynicism that fought against the hope all at the same time. She had said to come see her again, but after she "figured it all out," whatever the hell that meant. Another nearby flash of lightning and crack of thunder made up Annabelle's mind for her, and she ran out of the garden and toward Caretaker's house as fast as she could. By the time she got to the door, she was drenched from head to toe. Even her backpack was dripping. Stopping to breathe for a moment now that she was under the roof of the front porch, she wiped off her face and pulled her hair back, squeezing it out as she went.

Annabelle groaned out loud again, but without another choice, she opted to ring the doorbell. Given what she was sure was a very early morning hour, she knew she would be waking Caretaker up. After a few moments and three more hits of lightning, she rang the bell three more times. This time, she accompanied it with several bangs of her fist on the door.

A very disheveled Caretaker appeared, hastily pulling a robe over her pajamas. She turned on the porch light and peered out at Annabelle through the window before yanking the door open and abruptly pulling Annabelle inside. Caretaker then firmly closed the door behind her. The rain pelted the metal roof, creating a soothing melodic refrain that changed the tenor of the storm. The fierce weather was now a trusted friend, whiling away the morning hours in musical pursuits. Annabelle smiled at the sound.

When you turn around, you see Caretaker's face and are instantly reminded that you are intruding. You watch as more silver patches appear in Caretaker's wild hair, and wrinkles kiss the corner of her eyes. You've never seen it happen so quickly, so easily. Caretaker crosses her arms across her robe and ducks her head down, looking to the ground.

"Annabelle." Caretaker lifted her eyes back to Annabelle's face. The word is a mere acknowledgment of her presence. It wasn't an invitation to talk. It wasn't even really a greeting. Just a statement. When the Caretaker had made eye contact, she averted her eyes again, looking at the growing puddle around Annabelle's feet. "I'll be right back with a couple of towels." She brushed past Annabelle and moved quickly to another room Annabelle assumed was the bathroom. She emerged just as quickly with two brightly colored towels in her arms.

Annabelle held out her hands for the towels and began to dry herself off. She then turned her attention to the puddle on the floor, spreading a towel over it and stepping on it. She set her backpack on the other towel. "I was caught in the storm," she said as she straightened up to look at Caretaker again. "I've been spending all my time…"

"In the garden." Caretaker snorted. "Right. You've tried that line before, remember?"

"Well, this time, it happens to be true." Annabelle snapped at Caretaker. Tension, lack of sleep, and hunger piled on top of each other, leaving Annabelle's nerves frayed. To top it off, Caretaker's hair was now completely white, and the hands at her side were shaking ever so slightly.

"Is it?" Caretaker looked at her sardonically, then shrugged and continued, "I'm sorry. I'm having trouble with Raine, and I just don't have anything left right now." Even her voice trembled.

"You're having trouble with the rain? Like… like what? A leak? Cracked basement window or something?" Annabelle asked out of reflex.

"No," Caretaker laughed just a little, "Raine the person. You know, R A I N E. But here, let me get you something to change into. I'm sure I have some pajamas that will fit you at least while we dry these." Caretaker shuffled out of the room. She reappeared in a moment with some comfy pajamas. "These should work nicely. You can change it in the bathroom. If you'd like to shower there's a fresh towel on the counter in there." And she pointed to a white door down the hallway.

Annabelle took a long, hot shower, reveling in the water pouring over her. When she finally got out, she took her time patting her hair dry with the towel. She changed into the clothes she was handed and squeezed out her dripping clothing in the tub before bundling them up and bringing them out. Caretaker had moved on to the kitchen, which was around the corner from the living room and entrance to the house. When Annabelle emerged in the soft pajamas, Caretaker called out to her, "Straight ahead is the door to the laundry room. You can just throw them in the dryer! And then I've got some coffee ready for you."

Annabelle returned from the laundry room, and Caretaker held out a large mug to her, filled to the brim with delicious-smelling coffee. Her hand shook a little, so Annabelle hastily snatched it from her hand.

"So, how did you really get caught in this storm?" Caretaker asked as she eased herself into a chair next to a small table with her own steaming cup.

"I'm telling you the truth. I spent the day yesterday in the Writer's room, and when I came out I was so tired I just fell asleep in the garden —in a little spot hidden in the trees. I woke up to a flash of lightning that came with a huge roll of thunder." Annabelle watched some color return to Caretaker's hair as she talked about being in the Writer's room and then realized that she could ride that thought for a while. "Yeah, everything is really coming together. I've spent so much time with the Writer in the room he made for me. I can't believe how awesome it is! It's so different from your room—not that yours isn't great, of course. It is! But I can tell mine was made just for me!" Annabelle smiled and looked straight into Caretaker's eyes as she talked about it. For a moment, Caretaker smiled, and the wrinkles started to smooth. Annabelle could see the desire to hope dance across Caretaker's face. But in a flash, it was gone. Caretaker didn't acknowledge it with anything more than an "mmm" before she turned and sipped her too-hot coffee.

As the storm raged outside, Annabelle began to wonder about her plans for the day. Would the shipment to the other side of the Island even be sent? Surely, the Writer wouldn't send his people out in this storm. If he did, all hope was lost. There was no way she would make it across the island to her bridge to get her fake uniform and get changed in time for the morning shipment. And without that possibility, how would she ever get to the other side of the island? For that matter, how would she carry out her revenge on Pedro? Her future book said nothing about a storm on this day, and Annabelle couldn't help but feel like she was going a little crazy.

After a moment in silence, she asked timidly, "Caretaker?"

"Mmm?" Caretaker held her coffee in both hands, focusing on the bracing scent and the warmth. A yawn escaped her lips, reminding Annabelle of the early hour. It was enough to distract her from the question she wanted to ask for a moment.

"Hey, what time is it anyway?" She looked around for a clock.

Caretaker shrugged and yawned again, "I'm really not sure! It's early. Very early." And she chuckled a little. "It doesn't matter too much anyway, does it? You're surely not headed out in this storm again!"

With that, Annabelle snapped back to the urgency of the day and her question for Caretaker. "Right, yeah, of course, I'm not." The storm grew louder, seeming to crash up against the house with every wave of rain. "But I do have a question about the storm."

"Ok." From Caretaker's disinterested manner, Annabelle wasn't sure if that meant she should ask or not, but she went for it anyway.

"My future book... it doesn't say anything about the storm today. I'm sure of it. Has your book ever been... wrong?"

Caretaker smiled gently at her and stood. She walked over to a shelf on the wall and picked up what Annabelle knew to be a Future Book. Caretaker turned back to Annabelle and held the book out, spinning it side to side and flipping it over so that Annabelle could see clearly that the book was in pristine condition.

Annabelle's brow furrowed with confusion. She lifted a hand toward the Future Book, then dropped it back by her side. Understanding dawned on her. "You've never read yours."

Caretaker smiled and put the book back on the shelf. "That's right. I never felt the need. I spend my time with the Writer, and I read the messages the Messenger brings to me. That's all I've ever needed. I don't need to know the future when I have that." Her smile grew as she witnessed the shock on Annabelle's face.

"But! But! But don't you want to know what's going to happen to you? What if something bad is coming? Like, what if you're gonna die in a week or two weeks? Wouldn't you want to know that? Wouldn't you want to change it?" Annabelle's movements grew tense and twitchy while Caretaker silently watched.

After a moment, she opened her mouth again to speak, "I've found that the bad things come anyway, and knowing doesn't change anything. But I've also found that nothing is so bad I can't make it through as long as I'm listening to the Writer and doing what he says. And someday, when I do die—and we all die— that will all be within the Keeper's plans for me. Besides, what do you think happens after we die? Death isn't the end, and it isn't the enemy. But surely you know all this if you've been spending your days with the Writer?" She raised one eyebrow at Annabelle as she asked the final question.

"Well, yes, of course." Annabelle gathered herself together again. "So, you haven't read your book, and you don't know if it's ever been wrong."

"Well, that's almost true. I do know it isn't wrong." As she spoke of the Keeper, the Writer, and the Messenger, her appearance had shifted back to a younger version. With sandy brown hair now, she plopped back onto her chair and lifted her cup back to her lips.

"But, how can you…" Annabelle was interrupted by the sound of a door opening and closing around the corner. Before she finished the sentence, she was shocked into silence by the sight of Isaac shuffling into view, rubbing the sleep from his eyes. His soft blonde hair was all over the place, and his pajamas were rumpled.

"CT, what's all the hullabaloo? Why are you up so early?" He asked with a huge yawn.

"Isaac," Caretaker gave him a wide grin, and her face lifted, "Annabelle here showed up on the doorstep; she got a little water-logged in the garden this morning!"

Isaac stopped rubbing his eyes and peeped out from under his fist with a gigantic grin across his face. "Annabelle! Hi!" The thunder crashed around them, and it was as if Isaac had just realized then what the weather was up to. "Aw, you were stuck out in *this*? No wonder you got soaked! What were you doing out in this weather anyway?"

Annabelle was too busy looking back and forth between Caretaker and Isaac, dumbfounded, to listen to his query. Instead, she asked a question of her own, "Wait a minute, Isaac, is your one kid left in the house?"

Caretaker gave her an amused look. "Well, yes. You've met Isaac?"

Isaac interjected excitedly, "Yes! We spent all day yesterday with the Writer together. It was the best day *ever!*"

Caretaker nodded in understanding. "Another great day by the waterside, eh?" She looked pointedly at Annabelle, who stared back with blank, lifeless eyes, while Isaac enthusiastically nodded, "Yes." One silver streak found its way back into Caretaker's hair, but she closed her eyes and shook her head as if to rid herself of it, and it slowly morphed back to brown. Before she opened her eyes again, Isaac dropped a kiss on her cheek, and every sign of age fell off of Caretaker in a flash. When she opened her eyes again, they sparkled.

Annabelle hadn't been able to stop the lifeless stare, but as Caretaker's bright eyes turned toward her again, she fled to the sink and put her empty mug into it. When she turned back to Caretaker and Isaac, she had forced a bright smile onto her face.

She knew nobody was fooled. But nobody said anything about it either, and that's all she wanted. Mercifully, the next thing Caretaker said was a change of subject.

"Isaac, don't you have a big delivery today?" Caretaker looked up at the youth.

"Boy, do I ever! Liev and Adler said I could come with them to deliver the Future Books across the bridge! I've never been to the other side of the Island! I wonder what it's like over there. Can you imagine living in a place where nobody knows what their day will be like? Not just me—*no one!* What a crazy life that has got to be! Is it just total chaos over there, CT?" As he said all this, he bounced around the room, delighted with the thought of experiencing something so new and different.

"No, it's not total chaos, silly boy. Just because you don't know what's coming doesn't mean you can't have a pretty good guess. Although, I will say I was surprised by Annabelle's early morning visit! But, once the storm passes and she's all set, my day will go back to what it was going to be anyway; I will visit the Writer's Room, I'll go get the supplies I need for my next project, and I'll make dinner for us. At the end of the day, I'll be all cozy in my bed." She paused for a moment, tilting her head to the side as if to listen. The move made Annabelle very uncomfortable, as if the Messenger were in the room and knew her next steps. It only lasted a second, and then Caretaker continued, "None of that sounds very chaotic, does it, dear boy? And over on the other side of the Island, they only have as much chaos as they want to have. Just like here. People can cause their own chaos even when they know what's coming."

"Still, it's going to be great to cross the bridge and see what the other part of the world is like! I'm so excited they let me tag along today!" His innocent smile distracted Annabelle for a moment, and then the full import of what he was saying sunk into her soul.

"So, you're going with them today? Across the bridge." The thought sunk to the bottom of her stomach with a thud. Caretaker was busy looking at Isaac, and Isaac was too busy being over the moon for either one of them to notice the dread in her voice.

CHAPTER 17

Chapter 6–Day 12, still early morning
You sink onto a stool as fear winds its way around
your legs and torso and up toward your throat. All the
blood drains from your face. And just when you think
things could not get any worse, a hulking shadow crosses
the front window, and the door starts to open.

The crash of the front door as it was flung open shocked Annabelle. The fear that encircled her throat moved inward and down again to her stomach, making her want to release the coffee she had just finished. Isaac and Caretaker didn't seem at all surprised by the loud sound. The imposing figure lifted a hood off and shook out straight, blonde hair, and in that instant, Annabelle knew him to be her Protector.

Annabelle tried to bring up the next section of her Future Book, but she couldn't even see a vague picture of the writing in her mind. It was simply gone from her memory.

"Ian," the warmth in Caretaker's voice filled the room, "come to have something warm to drink! Some tea?"

"I'd love that, Emory," Protector smiled back at her, and Annabelle almost felt as if the rest of the room had disappeared for those two, "However, today... I can't. Today isn't a normal day." He turned and looked directly into Annabelle's cold, blue eyes. His own eyes burned with an intensity that almost broke through the ice of her glare. Just when she thought she would break, he softened and turned to Isaac. "Son, when you go out today, remember that there's nothing more important than following the directives of the Writer. And, remember..." He broke off mid-sentence with a catch in his throat, "Remember, I'm proud of you."

Out of the corner of her eye, Annabelle caught a look on Isaac's face she had never seen before. She couldn't quite place it. And she couldn't let her guard down long enough to try to understand what was going on. She did know, in a flash, that her plan with the uniform was not going to work. Her plan for revenge on Pedro was doomed. Even though she had been so sure this was the way to go, now, as she sat here in Caretaker's cozy kitchen with the fire of her Protector's gaze burning its way through her and the innocence of Issac's face printed on her mind, she knew it was all doomed to fail. And with the next flash of lightning, she saw once again the scene she had worked so hard to change.

A flash of light illuminates the blade in your hand— and the one in Pedro's. You're circling around each other, both knowing death is dancing in the circle as well. With a yell and a move too fast to stop, Pedro lunges, and his knife hits its mark. You can't stop him, but you do get a jab of your own in, barely penetrating his right arm. Looking down at your left hand, you see there is more than just rain dripping off. You drop your bloodied knife moments before you black out and land on it. You will not wake up the next day.

Only Annabelle didn't remember there being lightning and rain in the scene when she had read it before. Her head was feeling foggy and scrambled as she tried to picture the scene again, just to be sure. But she wasn't able to do that. Instead, she felt the next roll of thunder shaking her to the core. *I'm going to die today. But... I can't die today. I still have time. I still have time to turn this around. I'm just getting paranoid. Everything is going to be fine. I'll get my uniform from the bridge, tell Pedro where to wait for the truck, and we'll do this thing. Nothing is going to go wrong.* But Isaac's fresh face danced in front of her eyes, followed closely by the all-too-familiar now faces of Liev and Adler. And if their faces were familiar, hers would be too. *I have to change the plan. I can't join the crew at the Keeper's Court. I'm going to have to wait with Pedro.* But if she waited with Pedro, the revenge side of things was going to be even harder to pull off. She might be forced to choose between changing her story and getting her revenge. The white-hot fire of rage flared up within her. *I will not choose. Both will happen. Both will happen today!*

As you silently pledge again to have your revenge and change your fate, the others in the room continue their conversation. You're too focused on your inner thoughts to comprehend what they're saying until Protector turns to face you, jolting you out of your thoughts with his icy blue eyes breaking through your defenses.

"Annabelle," he finally spoke, "I'd like to talk." And he walked around the corner toward the living room.

As Annabelle followed him on wooden legs, Caretaker breathed in deeply and released the breath slowly. It was subtle, and Annabelle would have missed the move altogether had it not been for the shimmering of Caretaker's hair as it flirted with both silver and brown shades. Annabelle glanced quickly over to Isaac as well, who still had a strange look on his face, as if a shadow had fallen over his normally sunny countenance. With a final flick of her gaze back to Caretaker, Annabelle left the room.

Protector's back was to her and his head was bowed as she entered the living room space. With one smooth motion, he wiped his cheek and turned to face her.

In a feeble attempt to control the situation, Annabelle decided to speak quickly, "Protec—" But Protector cut her off with a cutting movement of his hand and a curt, "Don't." His voice was as terse and angry as she had ever heard it and she could feel the energy radiating from his tense muscles from across the room. She fell back into silence.

"You don't have to do this today. *Don't* do this today." His voice caught, and Annabelle couldn't tell if he was commanding her or begging her.

"I don't know what you m—"

"You know exactly what I mean. Don't *do* this." This time, there was no missing the tone. He was begging. Annabelle's breath caught in her throat for just an instant, and her mouth fell open. She had never seen Protector be anything but fierce and strong.

"Protector, I honestly have no idea what it is you're talking about. I'm just here to avoid the storm. Once it passes, I'll be on my way. I won't bother Caretaker again if that's what you mean! I know neither one of you ever wants to see me again." She tried to make herself look miserable and pathetic. Protector wasn't buying it, however.

"Put away the theatrics, kid. I've seen them all before. I'm not talking about that. You *know* that I'm not, Annabelle. If you follow through with your plan for today the consequences will be more than you can bear. You don't want what will follow; I promise you that." Protector was pacing before the fireplace as he spoke, gesturing wildly into the air. "Messing with the Keeper's plan doesn't ever end well for anyone! I know you don't understand this yet, but for my sake, for your sake, please. Please don't do this."

Annabelle decided to change tactics and tried to mollify her Protector. "Alright, I won't. I'll stay far away. You don't have to worry about a thing."

Protector turned toward Annabelle, then his sky-blue eyes piercing hers. "If you go today, I won't be able to protect you. I can't get in the way of the Keeper's plans, and I can't help you get in the way of them either. I will be helpless to do anything. Please, you'll only end up hurting yourself and others."

"What does it matter if I get hurt?" The force and passion behind Annabelle's words surprised even her. "Would you care? Would ANYONE care? If I'm going to die anyway, it might as well be today!" Annabelle spun away from Protector with the final words, knowing she had cut him deeply. The defeated look on his face was too much for her to take.

But as she spun, she ran straight into Isaac, who stood there with his mouth hanging open and a tear hanging off his eyelashes, about to fall. If Protector's vulnerability was too much, Isaac's was even worse.

For half a moment, she considered dropping it all. The plan, the revenge, all of it. But then Protector spoke up, and the slight opening in her heart slammed shut with his words.

"Go, then. And may the Keeper have mercy on you."

Annabelle stood straighter, wiped an errant tear away, and said in the cruelest tone she could find, "He can keep his mercy," and she bolted to the door, grabbing her backpack as she went. When she twisted the knob, the wind flung the door wide open. She stepped out into the storm.

Your anger carries you all the way down to the river, where you find the uniform you so carefully created. What did it matter now? There is no way you would ever be brought to the Writer's room again to feast on grapes and fish. That door is closed forever. You glance down at your hands, feeling the burn once again of the white mark on the one and seeing the emptiness of the other. Well, today, that changes. Today, you will steal another Future Book. You will rip out the pages and re-write the end of his story. Whatever his ending was, you will find a way to make it so much worse. He will live the rest of his life in paralyzing fear of the finish. Who knows, maybe changing the words really would change the story, and you'll get your revenge through his death. And just maybe, the same thing could work for your book. You can re-write your own ending. All you have to do is get across the river and away from the control of the Writer. Take charge of your own life for once.

For just the briefest of moments, Annabelle pondered, trying to read the notes from the Messenger. Liev and Adler wanted her to. Pedro didn't want her to. The Writer had even made a second copy of each note for her so she had a chance. But, of course, Pedro had ruined that copy. She could try to piece it all together, but that would mean leaving the Keeper in control of her life, and she couldn't do that. No one truly cared about her. Not the Keeper, the Writer, the Messenger. Not Caretaker, not Protector. No one. Isaac's face flashed before her eyes, but she shoved it away. She wouldn't let that gangly teenager get in the way of her plans now. She let the ferocity of the storm around her fuel her anger and fill her heart. There was only one way to change her fate, and she was going to take it.

You stand under the bridge and contemplate the sticky situation with Pedro. You need his cooperation for this con, but he also needs yours. And in order to get your revenge, you need to be able to get your hands on his Future Book. He never brings it with him. You'll need to work your way into his hiding place as part of the larger con. But that should work, it's where he will keep the Keeper's agent.

A bolt of lightning danced before Annabelle's eyes, but the thunder that followed seemed to be further off. The storm was beginning to move on. Annabelle looked down at Caretaker's pajamas—soaked through from her run in the rain—and the green uniform she held in her hands, with the embroidered ox on the pocket. It was time to get changed. A hunched-over Pedro appeared just as she finished changing. He had with him two big, scary-looking guys with large muscles and a lot of scars. Annabelle instantly dismissed them as mindless goons, but it was still good to have them since they'd need to abduct two people now that Isaac was going with Liev and Adler. Annabelle finished buttoning the top button and stood face-to-face with a livid Pedro.

"Where have you been?" He snarled.

"Right here waiting for you, scum bag. Where have you been?" She tossed her hair back with a flick of her head.

"You filth, don't mess with me today. I'm not in the mood, and your usefulness is swiftly coming to an end. Don't think for one moment that I couldn't handle those puny agents on my own. These guys are here to remind you who's in charge here." As he spoke, he gestured to the goons who now flanked him on either side. They glared menacingly at Annabelle.

"Please," Annabelle scoffed, "they're here because you're afraid of a couple of little teenagers with uniforms. And I don't know what makes you think you're 'in charge,' you little insect. My plan, my con. Now," Annabelle acted like she didn't notice the aggressive stepping forward of the trio into her space and continued, "Are you ready for your part of this?"

In answer, all three pulled out knives and ropes. Pedro took one more step forward so that Annabelle had to tip her head backward to see his face. The tip of his knife danced dangerously close to the green uniform, but she stared him down. After a moment, he gave a mirthless laugh and stepped back, flipping his knife in the air and catching it again. When the three turned and walked up the embankment, Annabelle stealthily grabbed her own knife, sliding it into the side of her boot before she followed. One goon reached into a bag, pulled out a long coat, and handed it to Annabelle to cover the obvious uniform until it was time to use it. She threw it on as they made their way to their hiding place.

There was a road where the passage narrowed to one car width under a bridge. In order to get to the bridge to the other side of the island, the Keeper's agents would need to pass through this spot. It was there that Annabelle and Pedro planned to kidnap one of the agents and replace them with Annabelle. It would have to be two kidnappings now, with Isaac tagging along. Annabelle didn't let herself picture his innocent face. Once they reached the bridge, Pedro stationed himself on the road above so that he could signal when the truck was coming into view. Annabelle would step in front of the truck in time for them to see her and stop, and the goons would force the doors open and pull the agents out. This low-traffic spot wasn't too far away from Pedro's hiding place, so there wasn't much chance of being caught. Still, Annabelle could feel her heart rate rising and her breathing get shorter.

By this time, the storm had all but stopped. She could hear the rumblings off in the distance, but the only thing left was a drenching humidity in the air. Annabelle's hair grew disheveled as the heat of the sun began to break through the clouds. A drip of sweat cascaded down her cheek. As the storm moved on, insects began to drone. Time seemed to stop as they crouched endlessly behind the cement walls of the overpass. Annabelle's stomach grumbled with hunger. Her muscles began to ache from the tension. Just when she began to feel as if she couldn't take it another minute, she heard the softest whisper from up above.

"Here they come!"

CHAPTER 18

Chapter 6—Day 12 midday
As you step out into the road, right at the point
where it narrows, you see the truck. It's close enough
that you can see the agents inside. The Watcher at the
wheel, curly brown hair flying in the breeze, and The
Comforter in the passenger seat, with his bright blue eyes
crinkled with laughter.

And between them, she saw Isaac, his face aglow with the joy of this new adventure. His presence still wasn't in her book; Annabelle was certain of it. But she didn't have time at that moment to ponder the omission. She needed them to stop the truck. She began waving her arms frantically and saw the moment Isaac noticed her and pointed. Adler hit the brakes, and the truck lurched to a stop within arm's reach of where Annabelle stood.

Liev was almost instantly by her side, grabbing her arm. "Annabelle! What's wrong? Are you ok? Why are you standing in the middle of the road like that, you could've been killed!"

Annabelle gave him the coldest stare she could muster. "Don't worry about me. Worry about yourself." And she nodded to the goons, who grabbed him from behind. She thought that Liev would have struggled, but he allowed himself to be tied up without a word. He just looked at Annabelle through it all, even when she pulled his hat off his head and put it on her own.

By this time, Isaac had also jumped out of the truck, and one of the goons lunged over to grab him. When he realized what was happening, he looked at Annabelle, eyes wide with dismay and disappointment, but he followed Liev's example and didn't fight the ropes. The goon finished tying him up and dragged him over by Liev. Isaac looked up at Liev and moaned, "Aw, man! I really wanted to see the other side of the island!" Liev simply lowered his forehead until it met the forehead of the young agent-in-training in a silent sign of understanding.

Annabelle watched the whole drama unfold before her until Pedro appeared by her side and shoved her toward the still-open cab door. Adler hadn't moved a muscle. As if he knew his role in this play, he stayed in the cab, engine running. Annabelle climbed up in the cab, closed the door, and dropped her backpack on the floor, only then looking at his face. Adler stared straight ahead, jaw set, but with a tear slipping down his cheek. He didn't say a word.

Down on the ground, the goons and Pedro had pulled out their knives and directed the Keeper's agents to move around the corner. Annabelle knew that by the time the truck pulled forward, they would have all disappeared from view. For a moment, the silence was broken only by the hum of the truck engine. Then Annabelle spoke.

"We're going to the other side of the island. You're going to get us past the guard at the bridge. You and I will deliver the books as planned, and then we're going to make one more stop. If you don't do what I say, you'll never see Liev and Isaac again. Pedro has them and he's not afraid to escalate if I don't get back with what he wants. Now, do you understand?"

A muscle jumped in Adler's jaw. "Annabe…"

She cut him off with a downward slash of her hand. "Do. You. Understand?"

"Yes."

"Then drive." Adler shifted the truck into drive and began moving slowly down the path. Annabelle shrugged out of the overcoat, revealing the carefully planned uniform underneath. Adler glanced over at her.

"So, this is what you've been working on?" he asked. There was the slightest hint of an edge in his voice.

"You wouldn't understand." Annabelle stuffed the coat into her backpack.

"Try me," Adler responded sardonically. "Why are you so desperate to get to Canree Nu East?"

"What does it matter why?!? I need to get over there. I don't have any other choice." Her words were sharp and biting.

Adler took a deep breath and whispered something like a prayer before he answered her. When he spoke, the edge was gone from his voice. "There's always another choice, Annabelle. Frequently, that choice is laid out in the messages from the Writer. Have you even opened them?"

"I couldn't. They were taken from me and destroyed." *That much was true, anyway.* She didn't bother to mention that she wouldn't read them even if they were still readable.

"Oh, Annabelle. Don't you know you can always go to the Writer? He's always available to you in his room!"

"Well, I can't get into his room. Not unless someone else takes me! It's locked, and I don't know how to get in!" The petulance in her voice rose with her volume and she let her chin quiver and a tear slide down her cheek. Even she wasn't sure how much of that she was putting on and how much was genuine. For the briefest moment, the taste of ripe grapes flashed across her consciousness.

"There is no way the Writer would keep you from his room. Ever. It's just not how he is. What do you mean you can't get in? I've seen the mark on your hand…" As his voice trailed off, Adler gestured to her hand that was currently clenched in her lap.

"It doesn't work." At the thought, the part she had allowed to be soft for a moment hardened like iron in her gut.

"Surely he... oh. I see. He sent you the key, but you wouldn't read them. Do you have any of them left still? Or remember what the early ones said?" Adler chanced a sideways look at her with hope brimming in his eyes, then darted his eyes back to the road once again. They were getting closer to the gate.

"Adler, it's too late. This is my one final chance to change the end of the story, and I have to try it. If I thought there was any other way I would have already done it." Annabelle kicked herself for letting that much slip to the concerned agent.

"WAIT. You're trying to change your Future Book?!? THAT is what this is all about?" Adler's voice rose in disbelief. *"Seriously?* Have you even looked at your book lately? Do you know what it says?"

At that, Annabelle snapped. She yelled, overtaking the small space of the truck cab, "I know what it says! Of course, I know what it says! I have been living my last moments over and over again ever since the first time I read them. They haunt my nightmares and disrupt my daydreams. It's everywhere, all the time. I can't get away from it! Why else would I be here?!?"

Adler sighed. "Listen, Annabelle. You haven't heard a word I've said since the day we met, but if you're ever going to listen to any of my words, I want you to hear these..." But they rolled up to the gate, and Adler's words were cut short.

Annabelle looked over at the gate agent, who was wearing a darker green uniform without an emblem on it, just a name tag that read "Amber." She was petite with fire-red hair and a bounce in her step.

"Adler! Good to see you! How's life on the West side?" Her smile changed her whole face, drawing out charming dimples.

"Amber!" Adler smiled back, "It's been an interesting day, I can tell you that. But on the whole, it's all like the Keeper made it to be, isn't it? It's good. And what about you?"

"Some things are no bueno, but I'm still here, still doin' my job. Speaking of, can I have your ID, please?" She held out her hand and

Adler placed his ID into it. She then looked expectantly at Annabelle, who panicked for a moment.

"Um, my ID?" Annabelle stammered and looked at Adler with pleading in her eyes.

Adler pondered for a moment, then slowly said, "You know, Amber, Annabelle here is a new recruit. She just put that uniform on today and hasn't had a chance to get that ID yet." He shrugged as he said it like it wasn't a big deal or all that unusual.

And Amber shrugged back. "Well, alright, if you say so!" She logged his ID in her system and handed it back to him. "See you later, Adler. And welcome, Annabelle." She waved and ducked back inside her booth to raise the gate.

As soon as they were out of hearing distance, Annabelle exclaimed in disbelief, "You *lied*. I didn't think the Keeper's agents could do that!"

Adler made a face but didn't respond directly. Instead, he picked up again where he had left off. "Like I was saying, Annabelle, I really want you to hear this one thing I'm going to tell you, ok?"

"Sure, whatever, *Agent*." Annabelle intended the last word to be a dig.

Adler sighed but continued, "You need to open your book today and read it now before we get to the Keeper's Court East."

"Uh, yeah, no, I'm not going to do that."

"ANNABELLE. Do it NOW." His tone was commanding, like one who knew he had the authority to speak.

"Oh my word, you sound like my Protector. Stop it." Annabelle rolled her eyes. When he didn't respond, she looked over at him questioningly. His features were set like stone, without a hint of his usual good humor. He drove in icy silence. She contemplated doing what he said, after all, she knew what it said already, so what could it hurt?

You continue through the elegant streets of Canree Nu East without even seeing them. If you had been paying attention at all you would have seen they were a mirror image of the streets of Canree Nu West. Instead, the bag at your feet beckons you to open it and get the Future Book from inside. But you know how today will go—success on all fronts except for the one that matters the most. And when you think of that, the rage is replaced by a dullness, a heaviness. You can't lift your arms or open your mouth to speak. You slump in your seat, and your clenched fists fall open, revealing a piece of the strange white mark on your palm. You curl your fingers in enough to trace out the marking, wondering about the "key" Adler spoke about. This leads you back to pondering the Future Book and why Adler might want you to open it again. You haven't opened it since the day in the Keeper's Court when you ripped out a page and received the mark. As you remember that moment, Adler's voice breaks into your thoughts...

"Annabelle, open your book." Adler spoke gently and persuasively this time, "It's not going to hurt you. I think it will help, I really do!"

Annabelle shrugged off the sluggishness and reached down to unzip her bag. Her hand easily found the cracked and worn leather of the book and pulled it out. Adler let out a sigh of relief, which irritated Annabelle greatly, but she still slid the book onto her lap and started to open it. Then, to mess with him, she paused and raised a finger toward him as if she were about to start speaking.

She opened her mouth and took a breath in, but Adler jumped in, "Annabelle! You seriously have to do this NOW! I've taken the longest route I can, but even you can see that we are about to be at the Keeper's Court. If I delay any longer, they will know something is wrong, so stop trying to mess with my head and just open the stupid book!"

Annabelle lifted her eyes and looked around. The truck was turning onto a street that felt eerily familiar. She could see a garden identical to the one on Canree Nu West, with the same statues rising just above the trees. She saw the Keeper's Court with its stained glass windows lining the top. And she remembered why she was there.

"Adler, listen," She spoke in a hurried tone laced with fear, "I'll open this when we get out again, I promise you I will. But right now, I've got a job to do, and there's no time. You need to tell me how the books are unloaded *right now*. And remember, Liev and Isaac are depending on you. If we fail here, I can't save them from what Pedro will do. So tell me, quickly."

"Aaaauuggghhh!" Adler howled with frustration. "Fine. We pull up to the back, just like the other side of the island. There will be a couple of agents to meet us there and help us unload. We bring the books into the back door of the Keeper's Court to the room with the gnarly wooden door, you'll know it when you see it. That's where he keeps the books until they're needed."

"Great," Annabelle replied as they pulled behind the court.

Adler shifted into Park and turned the key as Annabelle slid her Future Book back into her bag and pulled the zipper. They both opened their doors and jumped down to the ground. Annabelle pulled her hat a little lower to hide her eyes with the brim. They rounded the back of the truck just as three agents walked up.

"Adler!" They greeted him jovially, pounding him on the back. "But where's Liev? And Isaac? Weren't they on today's schedule?"

Adler shrugged at the man asking and gestured toward Annabelle. "Change of plans! This is Annabelle. Annabelle, meet the East agents, well, at least some of them." As he said their names, he pointed to them. "This is Mark. Behind him is Bonnie. And then over here on the left is Stewart." They all waved and greeted her and in return, Annabelle grunted a "hi" to each one.

"Alright, friends, let's get this truck unloaded." The one Adler called Mark unlocked the truck and threw the doors open to stacks and stacks of boxes. Then Adler and Mark together pulled out a ramp. All the agents began picking up boxes and handing them down to each other while Bonnie went ahead of them to the door to open it for them. Annabelle was the first in line behind her. Everything in the back alley was the same, it just flipped. The effect was disorienting for Annabelle, and she looked around, trying to re-orient herself.

Bonnie saw her face and laughed as she flung the door wide, "It messes with your head, doesn't it?! I remember the first time I went West. I had to get a map to get my head straight. But it really is just the opposite. Head down this hallway, and you'll see all the same doors. Keep going til you get to the wood one with all the nails and stuff. You can't miss it!" She gave her an encouraging smile that Annabelle tried to return.

"Uh, thanks. I'm sure it won't be hard to find." And she slid with her box of Future Books past the cheerful agent into the familiar, if flipped, hallway. When she was in this hallway in West, she had gone down the left side of the hall, door by door. She remembered skipping the old wooden one as she went so that that door would be on the right side of the hallway. Checking to the right, she saw the painted yellow embellished door—the one with endless fields of wheat behind it. Then, there was the gold door covered in jewels. *What was behind that one? Oh, right, the rows of shelves of scrolls.* Next, the mosaic tile garden scene with the sky-high white walls behind it. And then there it was, the knotted old wood with gnarled rusty nails poking out. This door made her hesitate as if there might be something behind it that was too heavy for her to bear.

Annabelle paused long enough for the next agent to catch up to her. Stewart, she thought his name was. He grinned at her and shifted his load so he had a free hand to pull the door open and nodded at her to go through first. Annabelle altered her grip on the box she carried and, taking a deep breath, moved through the open door.

She wasn't sure what she expected behind that door, but this wasn't it! It wasn't light or dark. It was more like the dusky moments of dawn—or just after the sun had set. Annabelle gawked upward where there was no ceiling. Just clear skies with a star or two peeking out. When she looked back down, Stewart was setting his box on a long, low stone bench. Annabelle followed suit, setting her box down as quietly as she could. The space had a hushed feel to it, almost reverent. She stood in the middle of a wide, flat stone, easily large enough for every box in the truck. Surrounding it were trees with gnarled branches and dark green leaves. The trees were much shorter than the ones Annabelle was accustomed to, with the highest of them reaching maybe twice her height. She didn't like this space. The quiet felt oppressive and heavy. Luckily, Stewart had already made his way back to the entrance, so she quickly followed him out into the hallway.

Once out there, she felt like she could breathe again. She let out a breath she didn't know she had been holding, then covered it with a cough when Stewart turned and raised an eyebrow at her questioningly.

"Allergies," Annabelle said by way of explanation and then lifted one shoulder in a shrug.

"I feel your pain! C'mon. Only seven billion boxes to go." They both laughed, one more freely than the other and then headed back out to the truck, passing the other agents as they went.

When they returned with the next set of boxes, Annabelle slowed her pace to fall behind the agent. The other three had deposited their boxes and had just opened the door to the outside when Stewart stepped inside the wooden door, leaving Annabelle the chance she was looking for. She paused for half a second and waited for the outside door to slam, then ducked inside the door covered in jewels.

CHAPTER 19

Chapter 6—Day 12, afternoon

You know you won't have much time before your absence is noticed, so you quickly drop the box and rip it open. Inside are several rows and stacks of fresh Future Books, but you're surprised to find that they're different colors, materials, and sizes. In Canree Nu West, they're all the same. You flip through book after book looking for one with similar pages to yours and Pedros. You finally find one with similar paper, but it's much larger and thinner. The cover is not too unlike yours either, with faded brown supple leather. You hold it up to the light and see shimmers of gold creating pathways and borders, almost like a map. You set that one aside as a possibility and dig through the rest of the books, but nothing else comes even close to the pages you want to replace.

A sudden noise in the hallway alerted Annabelle to the time she had taken going through the books. She stuffed the large brown book into the front of her uniform and tucked the shirt back in, hoping against hope that it wasn't too obvious. Then she set about replacing the books in the box as quickly as she could. It felt like years, but really, she was in and out of the room with the golden door in mere moments. When she lifted the box and pushed out of the door into the hallway, she was met with Adler's knowing stare. He was carrying a load in while Bonnie and Stewart were on their way out.

Adler leaned in and spoke under his breath, "I hope you know what you're doing."

Annabelle replied loudly with a high-pitched laugh, "Oh my goodness, how did I ever walk in the wrong door? I was just trying not to trip over my own feet!" And she headed down the hallway to the wooden door to deposit the box she carried. Adler wasn't far behind her.

"Annabelle, please, whatever it is you've done, it's not too late to undo it," he pleaded with her.

She didn't have a chance to reply, however, as Mark entered with a load of his own.

"There you are, Annabelle!" Mark exclaimed heartily, "I thought you got lost!"

"I did, for just a moment. Went in the wrong door!" Annabelle laughed again as if at her own foolishness, and Mark joined in. Adler gave her a pointed look and a heavy sigh before heading back out the door for the next load. Mindful of the large book in her shirt, Annabelle jumped to follow him out. Mark was just a step behind.

Annabelle made sure that Adler didn't have another opportunity to lecture her about her choices. She stuck close to Mark, joking and laughing with him as they unloaded. When it was finally finished, Annabelle jumped into the cab with a sigh of relief.

Adler sighed, too, and shook his head as he started the engine and pulled out of the back alleyway. Annabelle made sure he was occupied with backing the truck out before she pulled out the stolen Future Book and tucked it into her backpack. Step one accomplished!

"So, what did you do? What did you make me a part of?" Adler asked without looking in Annabelle's direction.

"If I don't tell you, you aren't a part of it. So just drop it."

"I hope you didn't mess with anyone's Future Book. You don't even know what you're messing with! That's not just paper and binding. It's somebody's life. Tell me, you left the books alone? Please, please tell me that." Adler's tone revealed how weary this day had made him.

Annabelle was already working on the next step of the plan in her mind and not listening to what he had to say. She started scanning the buildings as they passed for anything that might be worth stealing for Pedro. She wasn't allowing herself to consider what might happen if she didn't produce something worthwhile for him, and when Isaac's face came to mind, she shoved it away.

"Annabelle." Adler got no response, so he tried again. "Annabelle!"

This broke through her concentration, and she snapped at him, "What!"

Adler pulled the truck over to the side of the road and put it in Park, turning his entire body to face her before he spoke again, "You need to open your Future Book now. I'm not moving until you do."

"Do you think this is a game, Adler?" Adler began to shake his head in frustration, and Annabelle asked again, "Do you? Because I assure you, it is not. Let me refresh your memory. Pedro and those goons have Liev and Isaac held hostage. If we don't do what Pedro demands, you won't get them back. They'll disappear, and you'll never know where they went. And believe me, Pedro is capable of murder." At this point, she shuddered while the snake-like words slithered past her once again. She knew all too well his ability to kill.

Adler roared in frustration, "Why would you ever help him do this?"

"I don't have a choice! You don't know what it's like to have every move dictated by a little book because you don't have one. You get to choose! I'm stuck."

"But you're not..." Adler lost his patience at that moment. He reached over to pull Annabelle's book out of her bag but grabbed the larger one by mistake. When he saw what was in his hand, he dropped it like it was on fire. "No. No, you didn't. Annabelle!" The book dropped to the floor of the cab, where it stared up at her in silent condemnation.

Annabelle froze her features into a cold, hard stare. She wouldn't allow his judgment to move her away from her purposes. She wouldn't let him make her feel bad about anything. Annabelle reached down to secure the offending book back into the bag and out of sight, all while keeping her eyes trained on Adler's face, daring him to challenge her one more time. For good measure, she zipped up the bag and moved it to the other side of her legs, out of easy reach for him.

Adler grunted his temporary retreat, then asked, "Ok. What's next? How do we finish this terrible plan of yours so I can get my brothers back?"

"I need to find one valuable piece of art. Just one, but it has to be worth a lot. Do you know where we could find something like that?" Her tone was wooden, inaccessible, until the final question. Then she turned to him with a hot, piercing gaze and allowed her desperation to show just enough that it should move him. She had spent a lot of time perfecting the just-desperate-enough face. It usually worked.

Adler took in the change of tone and facial expression with a calm wisdom that went far beyond his young age. "Alright, Annabelle. I do know of a place that fits what you're looking for. But I want you to know that I'm only here because the Messenger gave me very specific instructions this morning, and I'm going to follow them. I'm not doing this because you look desperate, and I'm not doing it because I'm afraid of what will happen if I don't. Actually, I've got a pretty horrible feeling about what's going to happen if I do. But that's all up to the Keeper anyway, and I've got my directions. So, let's do this. We'll find the thing you're looking for in a gallery very near here."

When Adler mentioned the Messenger, Annabelle's eyes grew wide, and her face turned white. In all her planning, she hadn't accounted for the Three knowing anything about what she was doing. They just didn't figure into her plans at all! If they knew already, her chances of succeeding fell to below nothing. Despair washed over her. They would never let her use another Future Book to change her own or to change Pedro's. The despair fueled the fire of hatred within her. *Very well, then. If I won't be able to make any changes to my ending, I'll do as much damage as I can with the time I have left.*

Without stopping to think further, Annabelle tore open her backpack and yanked the stolen Future Book out. She flipped the book open and tore out three pages from the middle. The last time she did that, it had instantly burned a mark into her hand. Annabelle winced and slammed her eyes shut, preparing for the burn, but it didn't come. Instead, a feeling colder than ice wound its way around her hand. She dropped the pages and stared as a black mark emerged on her palm. It was identical to the white mark on her other hand in all except color. Terrified of the move she had just made, Annabelle snatched up the three pages and hastily stuffed them inside her own Future Book. The chill of the stiff pages made her shudder. Suddenly, she found she didn't want Adler to see the new mark on her, and she thrust her hand between her leg and the seat. She found with relief that Adler had been focusing on his destination and missed the whole thing.

"Here we are," Adler grimly announced. "Is there nothing I can do to convince you to take a different path right now?"

In response, Annabelle mechanically quoted the next section of her Future Book to him, "The Watcher pulls up to the front of a charming gallery, complete with water feature and gardens out front. He asks you to choose a different path, but you won't. You reach down for the door handle and swing the door open. Your feet feel like lead as you climb down from the truck and walk through the beautiful garden— although you don't really see any of it. Once inside, you peruse the collection, noting that there are several pieces of priceless glassware on display."

Annabelle paused here, recalling the motive for choosing glassware, and skipped one line in her retelling —the one that said it would be an easy piece to destroy once she had what she needed from Pedro. Then she continued, "You calmly take one down and hand it to The Watcher. The proprietor protests, but once he sees the emblems on your uniforms, his protests are silenced. You reassure him that the Keeper gave the orders and it will be returned soon."

Annabelle turned to face Adler and shrugged. "It's inevitable. Let's just do it." And she reached down to the door handle. Once she got on the ground, Annabelle started toward the entrance. But a small patch of pink flowers at the base of the fountain caught her attention. They reminded her of warm croissants and tea and whispered a story of love and care. And betrayal, Annabelle thought ruefully. A cloud scurried overhead, casting a shadow over her, and she shivered.

She hadn't realized she had stopped moving until she heard a whisper from behind and just above her ear, "What are you doing?"

To answer, she just pointed at the flowers.

"Annabelle? How did you notice the flowers if your book says that you don't?"

All the breath left her lungs in a rush, and her head began to swim. Every memory of every time something went differently than the book said crashed in on her at once, making her stumble.

Adler steadied her from behind, then whispered again, "Come on, let's go do this. Then you really need to open your book."

Annabelle nodded, and they walked through the clear glass doors together. Inside was a dazzling display of artistic work, with everything from glass pieces and paintings to statues and live displays. Annabelle could have stayed there all day, and when she looked over at Adler, she saw the same delighted and overwhelmed expression on his face.

"This never gets old." Adler walked over to study a particularly captivating painting of a fishing boat in a stormy sea while Annabelle got distracted by a smaller painting featuring her favorite flower ever —a sunflower—that was lifting its head to the sun. But soon, she turned and located the incredibly intricate piece of glasswork that she knew was just the thing for her purposes. She pulled on the back of Adler's uniform until she had his attention, then nodded toward the piece. He grimly nodded back to her, and she went to take it off its stand and hand it over to the agent.

Sure enough, a perfectly groomed, handsome young man came

bustling over to them, sputtering about how they could not simply take a piece! They had to first put in a bid, and... at that point, he saw their uniforms, and his protest drifted to a stop. Annabelle smiled at the man and assured him that the Keeper wanted to highlight the work of this artist, but it would be returned to him soon and worth even more for the exposure. As she said all this, she looked straight into his eyes, selling the lie with body language that went only skin deep, but he didn't know that.

By the time she had finished reassuring him, the proprietor was clearly pleased over the idea of the Keeper choosing a piece from his display to feature in the court for a time. Adler kept silent and simply followed her out after she touched the man's elbow reassuringly, told him he was doing a great job, and then turned to leave.

When they were once again outside, Annabelle celebrated with a laugh and a little dance. "Ha! I should've made myself one of these uniforms a long time ago! It's pure gold!"

Adler scowled at her, but she didn't notice.

"That was the simplest lift ever! That man was the easiest mark in all my life. What a fool!" She would have continued in her petty cele-bration, but Adler interrupted her.

"Um, yeah, so now that we've got this *incredibly* breakable piece of priceless art... what are we going to do with it? I can't exactly throw it in the back of the truck, and it would be pretty hard to explain at the gate back to Canree Nu West. What's your brilliant plan this time?" He didn't bother to keep the sarcasm out of the final question.

Annabelle stopped mid-jig and thought. What *did* they do with the glass? Try as she might, she couldn't see that part of the Future Book. It was fuzzy or faded or *something* in her mind. Whatever it was, she couldn't access the information, and they needed a plan fast. Annabelle scrambled in her mind to something she thought might work, with some luck.

"Here, give it to me and drive around the back of the gallery. There has to be some packing material they've tossed that we can use. Then we can put it in the back of the truck. Do you have any straps?" She climbed into the truck bed and then pivoted to accept the glasswork that Adler held out to her.

"I think so. Yeah, that might work." He slammed her door and bounded to the other side of the truck, climbing in with ease. Around the back of the gallery they did find some abandoned packing materials— enough to make the piece relatively secure. Once they anchored it with some straps, both of them once again got into the truck and set their minds to getting back to the other side of the island.

"Before we go, though," Adler mused, half to himself and half to her, "you really should open the book."

Annabelle, high on the success of their mission, absentmindedly picked up her Future Book and opened it near the back. Once again, her world began to spin as she took in what she saw there. Her mouth fell open, and she uttered two simple words; "It's gone."

CHAPTER 20

Chapter 6—Day 12, late afternoon

*A*nnabelle frantically pawed through the pages, finding as she did that only the last few pages were blank. Most of the book was still exactly like she remembered it to be. She shuffled through the chapters of her life, page by page until she came to the final chapter—Chapter 6. The chapter began, but she noticed, with a start, that the second page was the one she had ripped out so long ago. Annabelle traced her finger down the ragged remnants of the missing page. The page immediately after it was blank, and so was every page after that. The last words before the tear read,

"You're tempted to see the good in the day, but your doom hangs over you and won't allow peace to reside for long."

Fitting, Annabelle thought to herself, *That pretty much covers my entire life.*

She continued to slide page after page across her lap until she came to the final one. She could see the words describing her death clearly in her mind, but the page was blank—there were no words. Closer inspection revealed one small circular dark red stain as if someone had spilled just one drip on it. Looking at it, Annabelle felt like it might be a drop of blood. Her mind flashed back to the first day she read her story when she had run into the Keeper's Court. The Writer had been there that day, focused completely on the book he was working on. Annabelle could still picture the whole scene, including a drip of sweat falling from his forehead onto one of the pages.

It wasn't long before Annabelle realized the page under her finger was *today*, the final day of her life and the last page of her story. This was supposed to be filled with the details of her murder. Annabelle's confidence faltered. Without the words of her Future Book, she had no idea what would happen next.

"Why is it blank?" Annabelle's voice sounded small in her own ears. She reached one hand out and clutched Adler's sleeve.

"I don't know, Annabelle, but I know the one who does," Adler spoke softly.

"The Messenger," she whispered back to him.

"The Messenger," he confirmed. "Where are your notes?"

"Pedro destroyed them. He read them, and then he destroyed them. And he said the only way I survive is if I know what's in them." Annabelle's chin quivered, and she let a tear creep down her face. "Adler, today is the last day. This is the day I die in the Future Book... at least in the way it was. I'm out of time."

"Not yet, you're not. I'm not giving up on you. Come on." He revved the engine and pulled out into the road. "We need to get you back to the Writer's Room *now*."

Annabelle felt like time slowed to a crawl. Even though Adler was speeding through the streets toward the gate, the scenes in front of her crept along at a snail's pace. Every picture had a blurred frame surrounding it, but the inside was crystal clear. Each one came in between heartbeats. *Th-thump*. A child crouched down to pick a flower as her mother smiled at her. *Th-thump*. A shop owner is closing up for the day. *Ththump*. An old woman dropped her shawl and bent over in slow motion to pick it up. One by one, the streets slipped by until the truck was making its way back over the bridge.

Amber was still on duty there, still bouncing and smiling and dimpling. Adler spoke with her at some length, but Annabelle saw her like she was in a dream.

Finally, they were through and racing again toward the center of Canree Nu West, where the Writer's Room beckoned with every answer she needed. The wind picked up, nudging the truck over as Adler fought to keep it in line. And then the rain spattered on the windshield, startling Annabelle out of her daze. In an instant, she thought of the storm that was coming.

Adler was maneuvering down winding, narrow streets now toward the overpass where she had stopped him only hours before. Once they got past there, it was city streets all the way to the Keeper's Court. They turned a sharp corner, and both saw at the same time that the way through the narrow pass had been barricaded. Annabelle's heart leaped into her throat, and she felt like she couldn't breathe. This wasn't part of the plan, but there was nothing to do but continue down the road that went past the turn. Annabelle knew that this road led straight to Pedro's hiding place and that the opening to her freedom was now closed. The story had been set into motion, and there was no escape.

"Listen to me," she stared intently at Adler, desperate for him to understand, "the story has changed. This wasn't what Pedro and I talked about, but clearly, he's made a backup plan, so I can't get around him. This wasn't even in the Future Book back when there were words in it. It's brand new. I don't know what he's doing, but I have a pretty good idea. I think I can get you and the other agents out of here alive. But you have to do exactly as I say when I say it."

Adler nodded. He had slowed the truck for the sharp turn and continued on at a slower pace. The only way into town that didn't go through the narrow underpass was ahead. Also ahead were a series of tight roads and narrow alleys strewn with discarded furniture and trash. The darkening skies above them made it difficult to navigate, and he was giving it his full attention.

Lightning streaked across the sky.

Where they should have turned right, a stack of broken-down chairs, tables, and shelves filled the road. Annabelle knew that every road of escape would be blocked off. They weren't far now from the filthy alleyway that dead-ended in Pedro's hideout. He could make the whole truck disappear there. Annabelle's stomach tightened as it rolled into view. Pedro was standing outside with a drink, looking as if he had all the time in the world. His dark eyebrows lowered when he spotted them, and he reached back to press a button and allow them in.

Annabelle saw Adler hesitate and urged him to drive in. The doors slammed shut behind just as thunder rolled overhead and the skies let loose torrential rain.

When Annabelle and Adler climbed out of the truck, she could hear the pounding of the rain overhead and the steady drips of water making their way inside. Pedro met them at the side of the truck.

"And what have you brought to me, my love, my dearest one?" He reached over to kiss her, but she jerked her head to the side, and he ended up barely grazing her cheek. "It had better be worth the time I put into this." The snarl on his face belied the playful tone of his words.

"It's in the back of the truck. Glass is one of a kind. It should be enough to keep you at the gambling tables for the rest of your life." Annabelle feigned boredom and waved broadly to the back of the truck.

Pedro motioned, and the two goons appeared from the shadows by the wall.

"Go get this priceless work of art. And be careful." His eyes never left Annabelle's face as he spoke, as if he knew even at this moment that trusting her wasn't a good idea.

For her part, Annabelle took the moment to look around. She was hoping Pedro would have Liev and Isaac somewhere close, but she didn't see them.

"Looking for your good agent friends?" Pedro smirked, and the smirk deepened when she turned wide eyes toward him.

Adler broke in, "Where are they?"

"Easy there, agent. They're fine, and they'll stay that way as long as Annabelle continues to play nice."

At that point, the goons emerged from the truck with the packaged glasswork. They brought it down and began to unwrap it, with Pedro circling them like a vulture until it was fully exposed. Pedro breathed out an exclamation of awe.

"You've outdone yourself, Annabelle." He smacked the side of her hip in celebration. She barely kept herself from smacking him back.

"Can you bring the agents out now?" She did her best to look bored like she was just finishing up business, rather than what she really was: desperate, anxious, and invested. She was certain that her performance wouldn't fly past Pedro's sensors if he wasn't thoroughly absorbed in the artwork.

He paused, and Annabelle's heart pounded out of her chest. She silently willed Adler to keep quiet. Finally, he nodded.

"Sure." He tapped both goons on their shoulders. "Go get the agents."

The goons disappeared behind a metal door. Annabelle didn't dare breathe until she saw them return again with Liev and Isaac in tow. She heard the sigh of relief from Adler, too. Annabelle was relieved to see they looked unharmed.

"Annabelle!" Liev exclaimed and was about to continue, but Annabelle signaled subtly to him that he shouldn't talk. For once, he followed her directive.

"So what happens now, Pedro?" She turned to him with a hand on her hip.

"They're free to go." He didn't even turn to look; he was too occupied with the artwork.

"Just like that?" It was too easy; she knew she couldn't trust him, but what other option did she have?

"Just... like... that." Pedro got closer to examine the handiwork.

Annabelle turned to the agents and simply said, "Go!" And the agents moved as one toward the truck.

"But," Pedro drew the word out and then paused for effect, "The truck stays here." The agents collectively stopped and pivoted to look at Pedro. "That's the deal. The truck stays. And you never say one word about what happened today. Now you can go." He pointed to the door, dismissing them, and sauntered over to Annabelle.

The agents moved quickly to the door and out. Isaac turned for one last look at Annabelle before he let the door close behind him. Annabelle knew the clanging of the door was a gong signaling the beginning of her end.

"Why did you let them go? Do you really think they won't say anything? And what is the truck for?" Annabelle started grilling him just as if she were fully invested in the plan.

"That truck can go anywhere, and we've already seen your uniform skills have passed the test. Now, we have no limits to what we can do. Next time we can go over to the other side without any help. And I made sure they wouldn't ever say anything. I had some good talks with the agent and the little junior one while you were gone." At that, he started flipping out his knife and flipping it closed again. He looked too pleased with himself for Annabelle's comfort.

"And you finally did something right, Annabelle." He stepped closer to her with a predatory gleam.

"Did I?" She smirked back at him. "I guess that depends on where you're standing." And she purposely walked around him toward the glass piece. "So. Where's the buyer?"

"She'll be here any moment. And you'll let me handle it." He didn't bother to veil the threat in his words. Annabelle raised her hands in mock surrender and rolled her eyes. Then she sauntered over to a stool, sat down, and dropped her backpack on the floor.

"Not a word from me." She began inspecting her fingernails, doing her best to look bored with the whole thing.

A rhythmic knock at the door signaled the buyer's presence, and Pedro nodded at the goon closest to the door to let her in.

The buyer was a tall, well-dressed woman with tightly coiled hair.

The moment she walked in, she boomed out, "Pedro, do you want to tell me why there are three agents of the Keeper hanging out in the rain ON YOUR STREET? I almost turned around and left."

"Are they?" Pedro's brow lowered, and he continued darkly, "We'll take care of that."

Annabelle's heart started thumping hard in her chest. *What could they be doing? They should've been around the corner by now. They shouldn't be "hanging around."* The panic reached up and wrapped itself around her throat. She had to warn them.

In a flash that rivaled the lightning dancing across the sky, she abandoned all her plans. Well, all except the one that would work on her way out the door. She stood and threw her backpack on her back as she raced toward the door—with the glass artwork on her way. All it took was one hand reaching out to topple the piece and shatter the glass everywhere. The shrieks and yells of both Pedro and the buyer echoed in the empty room. Annabelle didn't bother to look back; she just bolted for the door. The taller of the goons narrowly missed grabbing the strap of her backpack as she ran past him. She made it out the door!

As soon as she made it out the door she started waving her arms and yelling to the agents that they needed to run! Instead of moving, they just yelled back that they couldn't leave without her. Two seconds later, the goons were out the door and chasing her down, with Pedro just a hair behind them. To her surprise, the goons both passed her by on their way to the agents, who stood rooted to the spot while Pedro reached for her. They tackled both Liev and Adler, and one of them grabbed at Isaac's arm, managing to throw him off balance for just a moment. Once he regained his feet, he looked back and forth between the agents struggling in the mud and Annabelle, who was locked in a struggle with Pedro.

Liev yelled to him from under the goon, "Go, Isaac! Follow the Messenger's directions!"

With that, Isaac sprung toward Annabelle and Pedro. He pulled them apart with all of his strength, throwing Pedro to the ground and helping Annabelle up from where she fell to her knees.

"Are you ok?" Isaac asked her, concern clouding his perfectly blue eyes.

"No, you need to go! You need to leave, Isaac!" She turned to run, pulling at his sleeve and trying to get him to move. But in those few brief moments, Pedro had stood and pulled out his knife. He grabbed Isaac by the shoulder and spun him around, expertly sinking the end of the knife into the left side of his abdomen. When he pulled it back again, blood began to flow. Isaac fell to his knees, then down on his side, clutching the wound.

Annabelle dropped to her knees by his side but knew there was nothing she could do. So she stood again, pulling the knife out of her boots and squaring her shoulders as she turned to face Pedro. Her angry tears mingled with the rain that flowed down her face.

And in that moment, it happened. The moment of Annabelle's nightmares, exactly how it was written in her Future Book.

> *A flash of light illuminates the blade in your hand—and the bloody one in Pedro's. You're circling around each other, both knowing death is dancing in the circle as well. With a yell and a move too fast to stop, Pedro lunges, and his knife hits its mark. You can't stop him, but you do get a jab of your own in, barely penetrating his right arm. Looking down at your left hand, you see there is more than just rain dripping off. You drop your bloodied knife moments before you black out and land on it. You will not wake up the next day.*

And she didn't.

CHAPTER 21

*A*nnabelle slept fitfully, heavy dreams invading the inky darkness.

She looked down to find a machete in one hand and a fistful of burning money in the other. Her clothes were muddy, and she carried a heavy load on her back. She felt a familiar presence behind her, and she spun around to look, brandishing the machete defensively. Behind her, her brother, Conrad, her Caretaker, and Protector, Rosa, and the sweet young girl from the shop stood in a semi-circle. Their tears had left dusty streaks down their faces, but they were no longer crying. Without a word, Annabelle understood that they were there to witness the end of her journey. Slowly, she rounded back to the path she was clearing and started swinging again.

The weight on her back grew heavier, but the work became easier. Thick brambles gave way to waving grass that fell with every swing. When she looked up, she saw person after person along the side of her path. Amber at the gate, Mark, Stewart and Bonnie from the other side of the Island, then the proprietor of the art collection. None of them would meet her gaze, so she returned to swinging her machete and moving forward. As she passed each person, they joined the group behind her, silent witnesses to her life.

She came to a clearing where Liev and Adler waited in front of her. Liev held a single black envelope. When she came closer, she saw that it had once been torn open, ripped into pieces and soaked in filthy water. Yet somehow it was together, and the single word on it shone more brightly than the sun: TRUTH.

Adler then held out a rusted key on a thick chain. Annabelle lowered her head, and he placed it around her neck. She expected it to feel heavy, but instead, it seemed to rest like feathers on her shoulders. The brothers placed one hand each on her shoulders before stepping to the side to allow her to continue her mission. They joined the growing crowd that followed behind.

There wasn't a sound except the ones that Annabelle was making: the whoosh of the machete sliding effortlessly through the tall grass, the clank of the chains around her neck, and, to her surprise, her own quiet sniffles as she cried. Her goal was still further away than she could see, but she persisted. She felt the eyes of everyone her life had ever touched resting on her as she continued swipe after swipe, step after step. After what felt like forever, she noticed that the light hadn't changed. The light hadn't dimmed or grown, and the source of the light never moved from straight ahead. But one thing had changed. A figure grew closer and closer. And behind him, a gate.

Energized by the apparent progress, Annabelle stepped up the pace. Swing. Step. Swing. Step. The rhythm built in her mind until she was just one swing and one step away from the tall young man with hair like golden straw and eyes like the sky. Isaac. She hesitated for only a moment before taking the final swing.

She stepped into the final clearing and straightened up, ready for anything other than the love she saw on his face.

"Annabelle," he held his arms wide open to her, beckoning her to step into them and be held. In his voice, she heard the same strange element she had heard in the Writer's voice when he welcomed Caretaker into his room. That moment felt so remote it had to be in another life. Despite not understanding, she dropped her load and fell into Isaac's arms.

Annabelle exclaimed, "You're ok! Bless the Keeper, he kept you alive!" She sobbed on his shoulder.

From above her head, she heard one gently whispered word, "No."

The meaning took time to sink in, but when it did, her arms dropped. "No?"

He shrugged and tilted his head, "Help came, but it was too late."

"And so..." she stumbled over the question, "So, am I? Am I dead, too?" She wrapped her arms around herself to protect her heart from the answer.

"Not yet. There's still a chance." He held out her Future Book to her, open to the last page. The stain glowed bright red. "When the Writer created your story, one drop of his blood fell on this page. It's there to tell you that this is the day of your choice. There have been many choices along the way, but this is the final one. You can choose to keep the story you have had, or you can choose a new path. The gate to that path stands before you." He paused, then spoke one more time, "Annabelle, I knew my mission. Are you ready for yours?"

Annabelle gaped up at the imposing iron structure in front of her. It was the gate to the Writer's room, but so much larger. The symbols on the top were too far above her for her to make out. Next to it, she felt insignificant and small.

"But I can't even open the smaller gate. How will I ever reach to open this one?" Despair swirled about Annabelle like a physical presence.

Isaac spoke again, as if from a great distance, "You have the key. Use it, Annabelle."

At that she lifted the key around her neck with just a glimmer of hope dissipating the darkness, but when she looked there was no place to insert it in the gate. She turned in desperation to Isaac, "HOW!?!"

"Not that key."

She spun around, looking at the mute group behind her. They all watched. Some with weary eyes and downtrodden countenances. Others with hope. Liev caught her attention; he was bouncing his heels ever so slightly with his fists dancing in front of his chest in anticipation. His face was lit up with the world's largest smile. She couldn't help but smile back at him. The one word on the card he held flashed back into her memory, and she knew exactly what she needed to do. She turned purposefully back to the gate and raised her hand.

She then raised her voice and spoke.

"I am Annabelle. I have cheated. And lied. And stolen what was not mine. I have hidden in the dark and kept myself from love. I have ignored the Messenger's notes. I have hated the Keeper, the Writer, and the Messenger. I have hated everyone. And I have hated myself. I blamed everyone but me for *the direction of my life. I hurt people. And I caused the death of the one person who loved me in the middle of all my hate."*

As she spoke, the elements she had picked up along the way began to change. The machete became a sword, long, elegant, and perfectly formed. The burden she took from Caretaker disappeared except for one book—the old book with worn edges that Caretaker loved. The money turned into ten golden coins. The chain around her neck grew into a breastplate of armor. And over that, the muddy clothing transformed into the uniform of an agent of the Keeper, with the seal of a crimson and golden ox on her front pocket. It shone brightly.

And when she reached the end of her words, she heard the lock clank and shift, and the enormous gate swung open to her. Behind her, there were cheers and yells and cries of happiness. She turned to Isaac, hugged him one last time, and stepped through the gate into the light.

A DAY LATER, Annabelle woke slowly. The first thing to break through the dream world was the sound of splashing water, followed by the roar of a nearby fire. She became dimly aware of a light flitting across her eyelids, and she tried to pry them open. Her vision was blurred, but she thought she saw flowers and rich fabric, and turning her eyes up toward the light revealed sunlight dancing through colored glass. She was in the Keeper's Court. As her eyes adjusted to the light, she saw the Keeper on his throne, but she noticed with a start that his head was tipped down toward her with a soft look on his face.

She gradually realized she was on a padded bench with heavy, rich blankets over her and the softest pillow under her head. She groaned as she propped herself up on an elbow. The Writer must have heard her because he dropped what he was working on and left his desk to come over to her. For the first time in her life, Annabelle actually felt shy.

"Annabelle," the Writer spoke, and it filled her with unusual warmth all over. She ducked her head, not from pretense or manipulation, but because she was overwhelmed with the feeling. He leaned over to her and lifted her chin. "Daughter."

The word broke open the floodgates of her dammed-up emotions. "I'm not! I haven't been! I don't deserve that name," the words were barely intelligible through her sniffling. The word, daughter, was too sweet, too precious, for her to accept when she looked at her life.

"Daughter," The Writer said again, "Will you choose to live in the truth? Will you choose to serve the Keeper with love like Adler, faithfulness like Liev, and joy like Isaac?" He fell silent, waiting for her reply.

She pondered the question, then answered quietly, "I don't know if I can promise all that, but I know I want to try."

Far above her, the Keeper nodded once and closed his eyes for the briefest moment. Joy burst into the deepest parts of who she was, and she laughed and cried at the same time. Then she gasped at the pain from moving her wounds.

"Well, as you can see, Annabelle, that is all the Keeper is asking of you." The writer smiled at her, and the motion crinkled the corners of his eyes. "Then we have just one more thing to do, but," he looked down at her bandages and trembling muscles, "I'm afraid you aren't up for a walk that far. First, let's pass together through the fountain, shall we?" He stood and held out a scarred hand to her. She took it, and he carefully helped her rise from the bench. It was good the fountain was only steps away; Annabelle could feel every part of her shaking with the effort.

She braced herself for the cold but, on the first step into it, found that it was delightfully refreshing. The Writer kept hold of her hand, and together, they walked through the heart of the fountain. Every step grew easier for Annabelle until she was practically dancing as they emerged. She laughed again, this time without any strain because her wounds were gone. From his lofty position, the Keeper laughed, too. The sound was that of a thousand rivers, a mighty wind, and a roaring fire all at the same time, and Annabelle couldn't help but laugh again with him.

When the sound faded away, and the Keeper returned his eyes to the things of Canree Nu, The Writer tugged on Annabelle's hand and said, "Come on, let's go!" He walked her out the door to the outer court and then out to the garden. Annabelle knew he was walking her over to the gate to his room, and her heart began to pound in antici-pation, and a little bit of fear. What if she still could not open it?!?

She didn't have long to wonder. They arrived at the gate. For the first time, the Writer dropped her hand. He took one small step back to give her the space and the ability to make her own choice. Facing the gate reminded her of Isaac and her dream.

She looked up at the Writer and asked, "Isaac gave his life, didn't he?"

The Writer nodded to answer her question, but his face was serene as he said, "Isaac was a faithful agent. He gave his life for the Keeper's purposes, and his reward is great."

Annabelle looked at him, baffled by the strange words. How could a dead person receive a reward? The Writer answered the question in her eyes, "There's a lot you still don't know, dear Annabelle. Be patient, and you will see." He gestured to the iron gate in silent question.

Annabelle looked back at the gate and lifted her hand. Then she spoke the truest truth she knew, "I tried to do things my own way and failed every time." For a breath, she thought the gate wasn't going to open, but then, to her great relief and excitement, she heard the metallic clank and groan. The gate swung open, and the Writer, with a huge grin on his face, invited her inside.

She walked down the stairs and through the door into the largest greenhouse she had ever seen. Row after row of green growing things greeted her, dazzling her mind with the richness. She bounced and ran through the rows, noticing brilliant flowers and lush tomatoes and squash. She stopped short when she saw the rows of grape vines heavy with ripe purple grapes. She fell to her knees in sheer aston-ishment.

"You have grapes here for me! My favorite!" She exclaimed when the Writer turned the corner and found her there.

He laughed at her blustery speech and answered her, "I know! They've been here waiting for you all your life! For heaven's sake, eat some!"

She immediately grabbed the nearest bunch and placed one in her mouth. She let her face show her pleasure.

The Writer motioned to a charming bench, inviting Annabelle to sit with him, and so she did. On the bench between them was a book that looked very familiar to Annabelle. She gasped, nearly choking on another grape.

The Writer rested his hand gently on the soft leather book. "This is your first mission, Annabelle. I'm sure you recognize this as the Future Book you stole over on Canree Nu East."

She nodded.

"This belongs to a sixteen-year-old girl named Chenille. I believe you'll find that her story is about to begin. But she is going to need this book. Your first mission is to find her and return the Future Book. I will deal with the ripped-out pages when it comes time." With that, he lifted the book and placed it in Annabelle's lap. The map lines glimmered gold on the outside, catching every ray of light in the bright greenhouse.

Annabelle felt the weight of the girl's young life sitting in her lap. At the bidding of the Writer, she opened it to the first page and watched in awe as writing began to form before her eyes:

Chenille's Future Book

Chapter 1—Day 1

Today is the day! Before you even open your eyes, you can feel the excitement racing through your veins. Every cell in your body is singing, "Today I get my book, my place, my story!" You have felt alone and adrift your whole life, and because of this, you hold onto the smaller kids around you with the fierceness of a mother bear. Right now, you lie in the bed you share with three smaller kids and one older one. You all used to fit without any trouble, but as you grew, it became a little crowded.

This morning, little Kenny's foot is a little too close to your face; you can smell it. You don't mind, though, as long as it means keeping them close. It is the nearest you have ever felt to having a purpose—protecting them. But the hunger inside of you has never been met.

You think to yourself that today is the day that all changes. Just holding your book will tell you who you are and who you're meant to be! You can't wait to find out what your book looks like! Suddenly, you can't take it anymore. You jump up, waking up the other four as you bounce down to the ground. They all complain or moan, but you won't be discouraged. You remind them that today is the day you ALL get your Future Books. Nobody cares quite as much as you do, but they start moving anyway. You do everything you can to help them look their very best with the limited resources available to you. You dig around for the least stained and wrinkled clothes for each kid and help them fluff their ultra-curly hair. You've been saving lotion for today, and you have just enough for everyone. You take great joy in erasing the ashiness and drawing out the rich and varied true color of each kid's skin and then your own. Finally, when you're all as ready as you can be, you take the smaller ones by the hand and lead them to the Keeper's Court, where you will receive the book that changes everything.

In your eyes, everything is perfect today. The fountain sparkles. The fire crackles. The flowers wink at you as if sharing your joy. The Keeper is greater, the Writer is wiser, and the Messenger is more beautiful than they have ever been before. The gathering here today is larger than normal. It seems like every kid off the street was there today, jostling for position. The Writer stands and begins to read out names. Person after person walks to where he stands to receive their book. The books are all of different shapes, materials, and colors. You can see how each fits the person and who they're going to be someday. The Future Books call out destiny just by how they look.

As each child receives their book, they go their own way. You smile and cheer as the kids in your crew receive theirs. First, little Kenny, then Angelica. Zane looked so grown up and responsible when he got his. And then spastic little Jazmine gets hers—it's bright purple with ruffles and sequins, and she loves it. The pile of books next to the Writer grows small, as does the crowd of kids still waiting. One by one, he calls out a name that isn't yours. One by one, the kids get their books and leave until there is just one book left. It is yellow with white stripes. You love yellow, and you think to yourself, how great it is! But then the Writer calls out one final name—and the girl next to you runs to get her book.

You stand awkwardly where you are, unsure of what to do. You shift your weight from one foot to the other and wait. The Writer looks over to where you are standing and calls you to come close. You think maybe he has just one more book somewhere for you, but when you get near him, you see the sad compassion in his eyes. He tells you your book isn't there, that you can't have it today, Your heart falls as you ask him when you will get it. He shakes his head and tells you that he's working on it already, but it's going to take time. The sunshine that filled your heart when you woke up this morning turned to stormy skies. Your brow lowers as you leave the Keeper's Court, vowing to find your own destiny...

ACKNOWLEDGMENTS

First, my husband, Chris, who waited for me to write this book longer than anyone else and pestered me every time I stopped writing. And loving me through the insanity. All my children for their courage and strength, and for all they've taught me. Rauri, who read over my shoulder as I wrote despite a passionate hate of reading in general. Calvin, who gave me great ideas for what should happen next. Akayla, Keziah, Keren and Frank, for their encouragement and enthusiasm.

Jen, for being my Samwise, faithful friend and sister. My mother-in-love, for the support and for finding the mistakes. My father-in-law for encouraging words even though it really isn't his kind of book. My mom for the late night phone calls and texts as I tried to process it all. My dad, for believing I can do anything and convincing me to believe it too.

Darla and SJ, who showed me behavior has meaning and who supported me and my kids.

This book would never have been written without M. Jeff Klingenberg's bathroom cleaning advice, the towel on Dr. Tom Phillips' bookcase, or Alan Kraft's last minute change of message.

ABOUT THE AUTHOR

Mary Ransome grew up in Grand Rapids, Michigan. She went to college in Denver, Colorado, where she met her husband, Chris. She is the mother of 11 children, 8 of whom are adopted.

Her hobbies are painting, writing, stargazing, and board games. She works as a CNA in a memory care unit. She's also written and directed local plays

Michigan, Colorado, Tennessee, Ohio, and Texas are all home to her. She currently lives in Texas with my husband and two youngest boys.

The best ideas come during road trips. The best writing happens in the middle of the night.